The Forever Green Leaf

LEW FROST

Llumina Press

ISBN: PB 1-59526-161-3
     HC 1-59526-087-0

Printed in the United States of America by Llumina Press

Library of Congress Control Number: 2004195125

Acknowledgements To:

Betty Talpey for her proofreading help.

My wife, Mary Lou, for her help, patience and understanding.

The parents of our grandkids, Suzanne and Marc Maki, Fawny and Ron Frost and Shirley and L. Scot Frost for raising kids anyone would be proud of.

The grandkids, Jena and Kevin Maki, Ashley and Nicole Frost, and Sam and Mike Frost for being part of the story. I'm sure when you read it you'll say to yourself, "I'll never need to do battle with a giant eel like we do in the story." But you may run into a big problem sometime. Something so huge that you believe there's no way you can win. The truth is you always control the way you think about things and that's what's most important to you.

All the Abnackis except for Red Feather believed the birch tree was sacred because it was so important to their way of life just as the way you think about things will be important to you. Would you rather think like Red Feather or Little Turtle? Only you can choose.

Chapter One

Troubled Waters

"Look to both shores!" Chief Graywolf whispered, as he turned to Broken Bow sitting in the back of the canoe. Broken Bow quietly passed the message to the canoes following. All eyes scoured the dark shorelines of the river. They were entering the territory of the Mohawk, their long time enemy! The dim light of early morning, and a gray mist rising from the water, made it difficult to see or be seen.

"Rocks on north side!" Running Bear called quietly from the second canoe, pointing his paddle at the swirling water covering dark masses just below the surface. It was the Moon Of Leaf Opening, and the Spirit Of The Waters brought dangers to those traveling the rivers this time of year. The melting snow and ice had filled the riverbanks. Trees, unable to survive the winter, had fallen into the river, their sharp branches blocking the traveler's way, hoping to pierce a wayward canoe. The young braves kept the knife edged chunks of ice away from their thin-skinned canoes with paddles while trying to stay upright in the swift current. Each year they made this trip downriver to the sea to gather shellfish. It was the only time of

1

year the water was cold enough to keep the shellfish from spoiling on the slow journey home when they had to travel against the current. They were proud of their skills and of the swiftness of their birch canoes, and looked forward to the thrill of facing the dangers of the journey each year. This year, however, would be different! This year they would face a danger greater than any the Spirit Of The Waters had brought them before!

"White water ahead!" Broken Bow called. The five canoes traveled swiftly downstream. They were approaching the mouth of the Ashweelot River and would soon be on the Connecticut. But first they had to meet the clashing white waters where the two rivers came together. The canoes slowed briefly as the river widened at its mouth and the towering wall of thrashing waters sounded like thunder just ahead of them. Then quickly the little boats dove into the foaming mist. The braves were now blind to where the other canoes were. Their paddles worked frantically from side to side, trying to keep the canoes upright as they twisted and turned violently. It was as if some angry white monster was trying to swallow the tiny boats. Finally the Connecticut turned green again, and Graywolf breathed a sigh of relief as he turned to see that all the canoes had made it through safely.

They called themselves the Abnaki. Graywolf and his men were from a tribe that lived long ago on the bank of the Ashweelot River just above Great Falls. There were thirteen tribes in the Abnaki Nation with villages of the Native Americans stretching from the Atlantic Ocean to the Appalachian Mountains in the place now called Northern New England.

The morning sun still hid behind the mountains, with streaks of yellow and orange light on low clouds in the eastern sky. Everywhere, there were signs that the long winter was coming to an end. A thin coating of morning ice covering the fields and granite outbreaks in the valley and on the hillsides sparkled against snow-covered mountains. "This is the mystery of the Moon Of Leaf Opening!" Graywolf said to himself as he watched the green pine boughs peek out from under the melting snow and new buds sprout on the other trees along the riverbank. "Everything seems to begin again! The bear will awake from his hollow tree and cross the valley looking for food. The river will turn white with schools of shad and the salmon will jump below the falls again! It is true that the Moon Of Moose Calling comes with much beauty...the red maple and yellow birch, but it ends with little light and shadows growing ever longer...with tree trunks holding only naked dead black branches. It is but an omen that the long dark moon is coming! The Moon Of Snow Blinding with its bitter cold and biting winds that one cannot escape as we hurry to beat the darkness, hunting on snowshoes the barren white crust that covers everything. But there is little to hunt and little to eat as the tribe struggles to outlast the dark moon. Now only the warm days, the days of good hunting and fishing are ahead. Yes, the Moon Of Leaf Opening is the magic moon!" he said to himself again, as they passed close to an old maple tree, its branches filled with buds. "This is the Moon Of The Green Leaf! The moon when the old is made new again."

Ahead, the Connecticut appeared to go between two mountains. The river narrowed and the current became stronger. Mountain shadows darkened the river and steep rock walls closed in on both sides. Huge rocks were suddenly sticking up out of the water everywhere! Graywolf raised a paddle above his head with both hands to signal the canoes behind him.

"Rapids!" he called.

As they entered the darkness the braves could hear the noise of the white water and Graywolf's voice bouncing off the walls all around them. They had entered the Connecticut Narrows, a treacherous stretch of shallow white water swirling over and around the boulders ahead of them! The young braves began to howl as their canoes dove and twisted wildly in the rapids, bobbing up and down like tiny corks in a stormy sea. There was water everywhere, smashing into the sides of their canoes and swirling into black holes, trying to pull the boats into their treacherous grip. Paddles darted this way and that way as they tried to stay upright, keep their boats away from the rocks, and stay away from the black holes. This part of the river was more than a match for the highly skilled Abnakis and one of the canoes capsized! The two braves in the water struggled to avoid the rocks and keep their heads above water. There was nothing their comrades could do to help as they watched their bodies being wrenched violently downstream.

Just as suddenly as danger had appeared, it was gone. The river widened and they were again in light. When the two braves were spotted swimming to shore, the hollering began again.

"Quiet! Keep eyes on the shore!" Graywolf ordered once again.

Silence came quickly as the braves remembered that they were still in the territory of the Mohawk! Graywolf sent two braves to recover the wayward canoe while the limp bodies of the two exhausted swimmers lay face down on shore. The canoe had been pierced in two places on one side but its structure was still sound.

"We will camp here and repair the canoe. Only a small fire," Graywolf said to Otter Tail who was already gathering fine roots for sewing new bark to the canoe. He started the fire while one of the other braves gathered pine pitch to heat. The rest took their fishing lines to the river where they baited their hooks with a mixture of ground corn and turkey fat and threw them into quiet pools near shore. The fire was put out as soon as the canoe was patched and the fish eaten raw. Graywolf assigned guard duties for the night. When the others settled down to sleep, Running Bear came to speak to his chief.

"I know we must gather the seafood when the water is cold to keep the catch fresh on the return but the river now is not kind to the Abnaki. We cannot be in the territory of the Mohawk without canoe!"

"You are right Running Bear, we should have carried the canoes past the rapids. We will not do it again."

"How far to the sea, Graywolf?"

"Only one day. We will spend two days gathering the shellfish."

Running Bear nodded and left for his bed beside a fallen oak tree. There was only the sound of the river and a baying wolf in the distance as the small chatter of the makeshift campsite grew silent.

At first light, the braves boarded their canoes and headed down river towards the sea. They felt much more at ease when they saw a Pequot runner on shore and knew they were past Mohawk territory. It was dusk before they reached the mouth of the Connecticut, having to carry their canoes around rapids on two occasions. They beached their canoes on the east shore of the river and Graywolf offered prayers for the group's safe trip downriver. The braves walked the shoreline, unable to keep their eyes off the vast expanse of the Atlantic Ocean that lay before them. A sight many of them had never seen before.

They camped in a grove of trees just off the beach, not wanting to be exposed unnecessarily even in the land of the friendly Pequots. They were a tired group and knew they had only completed the easier part of their journey. The difficulty ahead was lost in the moment as they watched the sun disappear over the horizon, coloring the crests of the ocean waves and the bottoms of the horizon clouds a brilliant orange. Darkness closed quickly and few words were spoken as they fell asleep listening to the constant drumbeat of the ocean waves washing ashore.

The next morning the braves were scattered along the shore busily gathering shellfish. Some dug for clams using wooden-handled bone rakes they had traded skins for with the Pequots. Others used large pieces of broken shells. A few simply picked shellfish from the ocean bottom and placed them in birch bark containers hanging from their shoulders. That night they put their gatherings in tightly woven nets and put them in the cold river water.

The next day was more of the same until the nets were full. At daybreak on the third morning the small band reluctantly left the seashore with their shellfish. For most of the morning the canoes made good time against the current on this wide part of the river.

"It will be difficult to work against the current when the river narrows," Graywolf thought to himself. "The canoes and the shellfish will have to be carried on shore often." His thoughts then turned to the Mohawk camp on the north shore of the Ashweelot River where it joined the Connecticut. There was no way to avoid passing close to the Mohawks to get to their home north on the Ashweelot. Graywolf always planned to pass their camp under the cover of darkness.

For three long days they worked their way north both in and out of the river, each night placing the precious catch in the cold river water. In late afternoon of the fourth day, Graywolf ordered the group to make camp. Once the canoes were unloaded he gathered all the braves together.

"The mouth of the Ashweelot is close. We will rest here until night and then leave so that we pass the Mohawks in darkness. You must all stay alert and be quiet. I will be in the lead canoe with Broken Bow and the others must stay close behind. There will be no fire tonight."

The men sensed the concern in their chief's voice as they dispersed to rest for the difficult trip ahead.

As he did every evening, Graywolf glanced around the group for signs of fatigue or sickness. He noticed that his canoe mate, Broken Bow, seemed worried.

"You alright, Broken Bow?"

Broken Bow left the two other braves he'd been sitting with and came to talk with Graywolf in private.

"Is it true that the Mohawk shaman commands a giant eel?"

"The drums say so, but I have not seen. Many command an animal. The Pequot shaman commands a red fox and our own, Manyfeathers, commands the eagle, Yellowbeak. It is the shaman's way to show their power. The Mohawks live on the river so he may command an eel, but I have never seen a giant one. But do not worry, we will pass the Mohawks in darkness and be at our village with the shellfish in two nights."

The noise of the river seemed louder in the darkness. They settled into sleep. A short time later Graywolf shook Otter Tail's shoulder who then groped his way among the braves in the dark, waking each of them. There was enough moonlight to load the canoes as they pushed off heading north against the currents once more. The Connecticut was still flowing fast and they twice had to walk the shore carrying their canoes and the catch. After some time walking the shoreline, Otter Tail motioned to the others.

"Stop! Look ahead! See the white water in the distance? It must be the Ashweelot."

The braves seemed relieved that they were at the river of their village even though they were still in Mohawk territory. They moved on foot along the east shore of the Connecticut past the foaming waters of the two rivers.

Graywolf whispered to his men, "The Ashweelot is now wide and slow. We will put the canoes in the river here and stay close to the south shore where the moon shadows are the darkest."

With the canoes in the water and Graywolf in the lead, they traveled quietly up the shoreline. They were almost out of the Mohawk territory when Graywolf and Broken Bow rounded a severe bend in the river. Graywolf reached into the water and grabbed Broken Bow's paddle to stop it and then pulled in his own. The others stopped also.

"It is too quiet. Not even the sound of the owl", Graywolf thought to himself. He looked hard at the shoreline closest to him and thought he detected motion, "Maybe an animal." Then a glint of moonlight bounced off something shiny in the trees.

"That is not an animal!"

Graywolf slowly pushed the canoe backwards and whispered to Otter Tail in the canoe behind him. "There is something on the near shore ahead. It could be a Mohawk ambush. On my signal we will head to the middle of the river. If the attack comes and they send out war dugouts, the nets must be thrown overboard to lighten the canoes. Mohawk war canoes are no match for the speed of the Abnaki canoe!"

Graywwolf moved ahead silently and raised his hand above his head. He lowered it quickly pointing towards the middle of the river. They had no sooner started towards the middle of the river than the Mohawk spears and arrows come at them like rain drops. There was the cry of pain and Graywolf looked back to see his friend Running Bear had taken an arrow in the leg. He glanced back a second time and there were only three canoes following!

"Throw the nets overboard," he yelled as several Mohawk war dugouts were being launched from shore. The Abnaki canoes quickly gained speed. Graywolf briefly considered turning around to try and rescue the braves in the overturned canoe. But the thin-skinned birch bark canoe was no match for a Mohawk war dugout in close combat. Graywolf motioned the group to keep going north, when Otter Tail yelled from the canoe behind him, "Look Ahead!"

There was a large area of glowing green light underneath the water and it was heading towards them! It began circling the canoes. The water grew so rough it almost capsized the rest of the canoes. Then right in front of Graywolf the huge head of an eel came up out of the water towering over the small canoes. It lunged at Graywolf who raised his arm to protect himself. The eel bit into his arm and threw him into the water. Quickly longbows were raised from the canoes behind and several arrows flew at the beast. There was a great splash as the eel once again disappeared below the surface and they watched the green glow move down river towards the overturned Abnaki canoe and the two braves swimming in the water behind them!

Otter Tail and Broken Bow jumped into the water and helped a bleeding Graywolf back into the canoe.

"You go with Running Bear," Otter Tail motioned to Broken Bow. "I will take Graywolf home."

They looked back to see that the war dugouts were closing on them. Otter Tail motioned the others to move quickly. Arrows and spears were now being launched from the Mohawk war canoes but in moving water they were not very accurate and none of the remaining Abnaki canoes were hit. After a short burst of speed the Abnakis looked back to see that the Mohawks had already turned and were giving up the chase. When they were well out of Mohawk territory Otter Tail wanted to pull the canoes into shore to attend to the wounds, but Running Bear had already broken off the arrow shaft sticking into his thigh and Graywolf had applied a tourniquet made of roots to his arm to slow the bleeding. Both men wanted to continue and get treatment back at the village. It was late the following day when the canoes came within sight of Great Falls. They were both elated and disappointed. Seeing sight of their home again was a relief but there was nothing to show for all the trouble they had encountered on the trip. Not only was there no shellfish, their nets were gone too!

"Take his good arm." Otter Tail said to Broken Bow as he pulled the lead canoe on to the shoreline below Great Falls. "I will steady the canoe."

Meanwhile, on the trail high above the falls, Graywolf's young daughter, Twilight, and her friend Sparrow, were returning to the village when they spotted the canoes. They ran back to tell the others who came out to meet the party. By the time Graywolf, held up by Otter Tail, reached the top with the other braves, the trail was lined with the entire tribe. There was a somber expression on everyone's face as they realized their chief and Running Bear had been wounded and one of the canoes was missing. Graywolf said nothing until he came to their shaman, Manyfeathers.

"Come to my wigwam."

Manyfeathers nodded and waited until Otter Tail and Graywolf's wife, White Cloud, had time to get Graywolf inside. He opened the deerskin flap wide so as to allow the eagle on his shoulder to enter without being hit. Manyfeathers was almost knocked over by Graywolf's son, Little Turtle as he burst into the wigwam before the flap fell closed.

"Where have you been, Little Turtle? No one knew where you were when your father returned. You must tell me where you are going!"

"Yes mother. I was fishing with Red Feather."

"Does Red Feather know that his father Running Bear has also been injured?"

"I don't know. Twilight came to the river to get me. I think Red Feather is still there."

White Cloud scowled at her son as she attended to her husbands badly damaged arm. Graywolf began to explain to the shaman just what had happened. Little Turtle was angered by the attack on his father, and seemed very interested in the giant eel.

"Was it really that big? Did it really glow in the dark? Did the other braves see it too?"

"Stop interrupting your father, let him finish!" Manyfeathers said, raising his hand to Little Turtle.

"I know there will be many stories in the village about what has happened and that the braves will be wanting revenge on the Mohawks, but I am troubled by that. We are a much smaller tribe than the Mohawks and if we attack their camp I'm sure many more Abnakis will be lost. The giant eel commanded by their shaman is bigger than any beast I have ever seen! With command of the eel it is no longer certain that the Abnaki canoe can outrun the Mohawk danger. Besides, I am no longer with both arms. It is not possible for me to lead the Abnaki in battle. I do not want the young braves inciting the tribe and attacking the Mohawks. Not until my arm has healed. I cannot even paddle the canoe!"

Manyfeathers looked solemnly at his chief. He knew that Graywolf was a fierce warrior and had engaged the Mohawks many times in battle. He did not know what to say. To not seek revenge would be out of the question with the young braves, yet he knew that this time it was different. Was it that Graywolf could no longer lead because of his wounded arm? Was it fear of this eel? He had to answer his chief.

"I will council with the young braves and tell them to wait until you recover. But now it is time for the tribe to offer prayers for our fallen brothers."

Manyfeathers turned to Little Turtle. "You have heard your father. You are not to talk about revenge. Not for now. Do you understand?"

With a dejected look on his face Little Turtle replied, "Yes."

When Manyfeathers left and gathered the tribe together, there was talk of revenge even as prayers were being said.

Meanwhile Little Turtle rushed to the river, where he had left his friend Red Feather, fishing several rocks out in deeper water.

"Red Feather, your father has returned and he's been wounded by the Mohawks!"

Red Feather dropped his line and jumped quickly from rock to rock till he was on shore.

"Is he hurt badly?"

"I don't think so. Graywolf said it was a leg wound."

"We must have revenge on the Mohawks," Red Feather said through gritted teeth.

"I must tell you more." They both sat down as Little Turtle retold his father's story and dwelt for some time on the giant eel commanded by the Mohawks. "But we cannot ask the others to attack the Mohawks. I had to promise Manyfeathers."

"Why? We have to attack the Mohawks!"

Little Turtle just shrugged his shoulders not knowing how to answer his friend. "My father has been wounded also. I know there must be revenge, but I had to promise!"

The two boys walked back to Red Feather's wigwam. His father, Running Bear was sitting outside the wigwam. There were tears running down his face. Red Feather looked at his father's leg and could see that the arrow had already been removed and the wound treated, but the pain in his fathers face bothered him.

As time went on, talk of the giant eel put fear into the tribesmen and there was less and less talk about revenge from the braves. No one wanted to move against the Mohawks without the leadership of their chief, Graywolf, who had always led them into battle. Little Turtle spoke about revenge to his father but Graywolf did not regain the use of his arm and would not answer him. Little Turtle and Red Feather continued to talk to each other and grew more frustrated.

"We must do something, Red Feather. There is nothing to stop us. We only promised not to get the others to attack!"

"But we are too young, Little Turtle. If our fathers could not kill the beast then how are we going to?"

"Then we must promise that when we are older we will kill the giant eel! The boys agreed to meet at a cave they'd discovered near the foot of Soonapee Mountain where they would make a secret pact to destroy the giant eel!

Red Feather entered the cave first carrying small twigs for a fire. There was barely enough light to see as Little Turtle made a pile of wood shavings with his bone knife. Red Feather spun a pointed stick in the shavings as Little Turtle blew on the pile of shavings. In time smoke began to rise from the pile and soon after there was fire. He sat against the cave wall and spoke to his friend

"I know you have spoken to your father many times about the eel. Could you tell me more about it?"

"It is difficult to speak of it. I will make a picture." Little Turtle pulled a pouch of ground red corn from his belt and spilled some on a flat rock. He mixed a paste with his own saliva and began drawing on the cave wall with it using a sharp stick. When the drawing was finished he stepped back so Red Feather could see. "That is what my father saw."

Red Feather's mouth dropped open. "You think it is really that big? And who are the two braves in the canoe attacking it?"

"Yes, that is how Graywolf described it and he would not make the eel bigger than it is. We are the two braves destroying the eel when we are older."

Red Feather looked pale as he watched Little Turtle take the bone knife and prick his finger until it bled. Little Turtle passed the knife to him and Red Feather reluctantly did the same. Then the two pressed their bleeding fingers together and Little Turtle spoke.

"The Mohawk giant eel will be destroyed by the Little Turtle and Red Feather to remove our fathers shame and have revenge on the Mohawks! Do you agree, Red Feather?"

"Yes," Red Feather replied in a low voice.

Chapter Two

Spirits Without Eyes

In the darkness just before dawn, Little Turtle was awakened by the "who...who" of an owl, a signal from Red Feather that it was time to go fishing. Little Turtle sat up and rubbed his eyes, listening for the sound again to make sure he wasn't dreaming.

"Wake up!" cried an exasperated voice from outside. Quickly throwing off the bearskin that covered him, Little Turtle put on his moccasins and then straightened the loincloth that hung from the belt holding up his leggings. After pulling the deerskin shirt over his head, he put on a headband and groped in the darkness for his pouch of bait and fishing line.

There was another even louder "Wake up!" as Little Turtle exited the wigwam.

"I'm ready," Little Turtle replied in much too loud a voice for his friend.

"Shhh! Is she sleeping?"

"I think so...I didn't look."

Red Feather never wanted to take Little Turtle's sister Twilight fishing. They didn't catch many fish when she was there.

"She's always talking! Scares the fish! And you have to be quiet too. Both of you talk too much! You'll have to walk faster Little Turtle or it will be light by the time we get to the river!"

Little Turtle was still trying to fully wake himself and paid no attention to his friend. Besides, he'd heard it all before many times. He reached for the calf of his right leg and felt the outline of his bone knife. He was glad it was there or his friend would have had more to complain about. They walked a short distance south along the trail to the river just above the falls. In the darkness there was only the roar of falling water and the occasional splash of a fish jumping. Before heading onto the rocks the two boys baited their bone hooks with a corn paste. Red Feather then moved rock by rock as far out in the river as possible. Little Turtle was less daring. As he jumped onto the third rock still wet from the dampness of night air his moccasins slid underfoot and he tumbled into the water.

"You're so clumsy! ...Now you've scared the fish! You can't even stand on a rock!"

At that point Little Turtle wondered why he called Red Feather his friend as he carefully climbed onto the third rock and sat down to check that he still had his line, the pouch of bait and his knife. Shivering from being wet he threw his line into the water and then held it between his teeth and folded his arms together to try and keep warm.

They fished in silence for some time until Little Turtle's line tightened suddenly almost pulling him off the rock again. He quickly transferred the line to his hand and yelled to Red Feather,

"Got one!" he whispered as loud as he could to his friend. Little Turtle felt a strong pull on the other end.

"Must be a bass," he thought to himself. As the two struggled, Little Turtle felt his feet slipping on the rock again and began letting the line back out hoping the fish would tire. The fish rose out of the water several times shaking itself violently trying to rid itself of the hook only to splash back into the river tail first. Gradually the pull weakened and slowly Little Turtle wound in again. When he pulled the fish close to the rock he could see the silver body of a large bass still fighting in the dark water. Fearing the weight of the fish might break his line he decided to try to reach into the river and grab the line close to the fish's mouth. As his hand reached the cold water his feet slipped again. He could not recover his balance and went back into the water!

Red Feather's voice echoed up and down the river, "Did you fall in again?"

To add to his embarrassment he pulled on the line and felt nothing! The fish was gone! Little Turtle climbed back onto the rock, baited his hook again and never answered his friend.

"How can you be a great warrior and kill the giant eel when you can't even stand on a rock?"

That was more than Little Turtle could take. "I will kill the eel and you will help! The spirits will be with us. We are right to seek revenge on the Mohawks! Remember our pledge!" Little Turtle said in an angry voice.

Red Feather knew that his friend was seldom angry and that he had gone too far.

He wished he hadn't mentioned the eel. "Perhaps with time he will forget!" Red Feather thought.

They fished in silence until the sun rose above the mountains. Little Turtle looked back at his village. There were many dome shaped wigwams covered with birch bark and animal skins. Smoke was rising from some of them. The rest of the riverbank was crowded with dew covered white birch and green pines that sparkled in the sun The campsite was a beehive of activity. Old and young were grinding corn in hollowed stones and stretching animal hides, while others carried heavy skin buckets of water from the river. A few canoes were beginning to make their way up river to check the animal traps. On the riverbank were several young braves. These were the warm days, a reminder that the Moon Of Moose Calling would follow soon and the nights would grow colder. The leaves will turn red and gold, then brown and fall from the trees.

The river was wide above the falls and looked quiet from the shore, but the middle was deep and the current there moved swiftly over the falls. Young braves were constantly being warned about the danger of being caught in the swift current and carried over the falls.

Now Red Feather noticed the young braves on shore. He put down his fishing line, removed his shirt and untied the leggings from his belt. He dove off the rock and began swimming towards the middle of the river.

"Where are you going?" Little Turtle shouted at him.

Red Feather did not answer but kept swimming.

"You're too close to the falls. I'll be picking your bones off the rocks below!"

Again there was no response from Red Feather. Little Turtle shook his head and sat down on the rock he'd been standing on. He heard hollering and saw that the braves on shore had noticed Red Feather.

"Great!" thought Little Turtle, "That's just what he wants, everyone noticing him! Now he'll surely kill himself!"

"Come back!" he yelled at the top of his voice.

Red Feather swam into the swift current and you could see his body being pulled closer to the falls. Red Feathers strokes quickened. He was far out in the river and his head barely visible above the rushing water. Little Turtle put his head in his hands not wanting to look at what was happening!

The braves hollering on shore grew louder. Little Turtle looked up to see that Red Feather had reached the quiet water on the other side and was leaning against a large rock, catching his breath. There was more clapping and yelling as Red Feather waved to the braves.

"Do it again!" One of the braves shouted.

Red Feather left the rock and began swimming back. Little Turtle decided to watch this time and not bury his head. He slipped of his rock and began walking in the water. He knew Red Feather would be more tired on the trip back. Little Turtle was now up to his neck in the water watching Red Feathers body being dragged even closer to the falls. Little Turtle walked towards the falls to be in line with Red Feather's course. Red Feather was struggling. His arms almost flailing in the water! Little Turtle was now just over his head at the edge of the swift current as he reached and grabbed one of Red Feather's arms and pulled him into the quiet water! Red Feather was out of breath and the two said nothing as they waded back to one of the large rocks they'd been fishing from.

Red Feather was exhausted and breathing hard as the other braves hollered for more. He kept waving back at them but said nothing to Little Turtle. After a short rest he began wading back out into the river.

Little Turtle was right behind him. "No more!"

"You going to stop me?"

"Yes!" Little Turtle came at Red Feather from behind, locking his arms around his chest in a bear hug. The two struggled for some time while there was more hollering from the braves on shore. Red Feather took them both under water several times but Little Turtle never released his grip. At last he felt Red Feathers body go limp.

"Enough?" ittle Turtle asked.

"Yes," Red Feather replied gasping for breath.

The two walked slowly back to the rock and collapsed in the water with their backs against it. After a time Red Feather smiled and gently pushed his friend s shoulder until he fell over.

"That was Red Feather," Little Turtle thought to himself. "Quick to anger and quick to let it go, but always wanting the attention of others."

"You cannot challenge the Spirit Of The Waters, Red Feather. We will need all the spirits when we attack the eel."

Red Feather took a scoop of water in one hand and let it drip through his fingers back into the river. "It is only water. There is no spirit! I believe only those with eyes and beating hearts have spirits. But it makes no difference, we cannot defeat the eel!"

"You are the only brave that does not believe, Red Feather! You know that the river has flooded our homes and killed the Abnacki! And it provides the fish we eat! You must show respect. And we will kill the eel!"

Little Turtle did not like what he heard from his friend. "Why was he now saying they could not defeat the eel. Perhaps it is because he does not believe in the powerful spirits that do not have eyes or a beating heart. I must convince him," he thought.

The two boys walked the trail home, ignoring the other braves on the riverbank. The other braves continued chanting for Red Feather to go back and challenge the river.

"They will be fishing for salmon tonight below the falls, do you want to go?" Little Turtle asked.

"When they use the torches to attract the salmon it gets too smoky below the falls. But the torches will light the sky so we can fish above the falls. Meet you at the river"

Little Turtle nodded in agreement as the two parted company.

That night Red Feather had been fishing for some time when he heard footsteps in the darkness behind him. "That you, Little Turtle? You alone?"

"No, Twilight is with me."

"I told you not to bring her!"

"Couldn't help it she hadn't gone to bed yet."

"I'll be quiet, Red Feather," Twilight's small voice shot back.

Red Feather just grunted knowing Twilight couldn't possibly keep quiet for any length of time.

Twilight stood on a large rock with her brother, not as far out in the river as Red Feather. Little Turtle had trouble throwing his line out with his sister in the way and the two began arguing about it.

"Will you two keep quiet?" Red Feather whispered as loud as he could.

All was still until there was a flash of light above the mountains to the east followed by a distant rumble. The night sky was full of clouds, hiding the moon and stars. Their only light was from the torches of the other braves salmon fishing. The flashes of lightening got brighter and the thunder louder, but neither boy stopped fishing. It began to rain and a few drops turned into a downpour. Then together came a brilliant flash of light and crash of thunder!

The lightening seemed to be right on top of them! Twilight squealed and the three of them were now scrambling to get off the river.

"Don't be afraid," Red Feather laughed. "It is only the wind bringing rain for our crops. The wind won't hurt you."

He could see that Twilight was not amused. With the rain pelting down on them, Red Feather raised his arms up to the sky and shouted "Oh Spirit Of The Wind, you cannot harm us! We are invincible!" And then began to laugh.

"You should not taunt the spirits, Red Feather", Little Turtle replied as his sister nodded in agreement.

Then another loud flash closely followed by a loud crash of thunder!

"See, you have made the Spirit Of The Wind angry!" Twilight shouted as loud as she could.

"But nothing happened to me! I am stronger than the spirit. It is only wind and the wind cannot hurt us."

"Look over there," Little Turtle said pointing to the hillside above the riverbank. The lightening had started a fire in the woods. "Can't hurt us? It can burn our crops and our village!"

Red Feather was no longer laughing as the thunder and lightening now seemed to be all around them. The three ran up the bank and into the woods together trying to get away from the storm. They ran through patches of high grasses and trees, the low branches whipping against their legs and faces. They came to a clearing and stopped waiting for the next flash of lightening to help tell them where they were. There were deer and small animals darting this way and that, frightened by the lightening and loud noise.

"Where are we?" Twilight asked

"Don't know!" Red Feather responded.

"I think we're close to the cave. It's over that way." Little Turtle said pointing towards the mountain foot-hills in front of them. He started to walk in that direction and the two others reluctantly followed.

"Why don't we just go home?" Twilight asked.

"Not sure we can find our way in the dark," Little Turtle answered.

"I think I see it!" Red Feather said excitedly, "It's right over there!"

When they got to the cave, Twilight was reluctant to go inside. "What if there's a bear in there?"

"We've been in this cave and there's nothing inside. Besides we need to get out of the rain!" her brother replied.

Twilight finally followed the two boys inside the cave. It was pitch dark and Twilight offered,

"I can't see! This is too scary!" and made her way back out through the dim light in the cave opening.

"I can't let her outside by herself!" Little Turtle grunted as he also made his way outside. "I'll stay with you, Twilight."

The rain continued. As the night air grew colder, Twilight decided to go back in the cave and stay close to the entrance. Her brother was glad she did.

When morning finally came, the rain had stopped and a column of light was streaming in through the entrance.

"What is that?" Twilight exclaimed. But no one answered. The two boys were sleeping soundly. She shook her brother, "Wake up! What is that on the cave wall?"

Little Turtle rubbed his eyes and looked at his sister. "What?"

"The picture on the wall! What is it? A snake?"

"No. Have you heard father talk about the Mohawks' attack when they went to the sea for shellfish? That is the eel that attacked them and injured father's arm"

Red Feather woke and overheard Little Turtle. "Don't tell anymore! It's supposed to be a secret! If you tell Twilight everyone will know!"

"You have to promise not to tell, Twilight!"

"If you don't tell me about it then I will tell!" Twilight shot back.

Little Turtle finished telling her about the eel and their pledge to kill it to avenge the attack of the Mohawks on their fathers.

"If she tells then the pledge is broken!" Red Feather said.

Little Turtle did not speak but thought about his problems. He would have to make sure his sister did not tell any of her friends and break the pledge with Red Feather. He was concerned too that Red Feather had laughed at the Spirit Of The Water and the Spirit Of The Wind and they might not help when attacking the eel.

Shouting outside the cave interrupted his thoughts. Red Feather went to the entrance and looked outside.

"It's Otter Tail! They must be looking for us. We can't let them find the cave!"

Little Turtle cupped his hand over Twilight's mouth until Otter Tail s shouts were further away. He then led his sister outside and the three walked away from the cave.

"Not a word about the cave to anyone, Twilight!" Little Turtle said shaking his fist at his sister.

Twilight could see that her normally friendly brother was very serious and simply nodded in agreement.

"Over here! We're over here!" Red Feather shouted.

"Found them!" they heard Otter Tail yell.

Soon they spotted Running Bear, Graywolf and Broken Bow with Otter Tail walking towards them.

"Why did you not come home?" Graywolf asked his children.

"We took shelter in the storm, Father. It was raining too hard to find our way," Little Turtle offered.

"You alright, Red Feather?" Running Bear asked. "There was a lot of lightening in the storm."

"I'm ok, just wet from the rain last night."

The group headed south, back to the trail along the river. Graywolf spotted a burned area to the north.

"Must be the lightening strike we saw last night. Come, let us look closer."

When they arrived at the blackened stand of trees, the burnt smell was very heavy and here and there smoke was still rising from patches on the ground.

"A birch!" Running Bear said excitedly, "Over there!"

The group immediately moved to the small, blackened tree and knelt beside it, all except Red Feather.

There was silence for a moment and then Graywolf said a prayer wishing the spirit of the tree a long life. Running Bear saw that his son did not offer a prayer to the tree and became very angry.

"Son, why do you not pray? I have watched you pray for the spirit of the fallen caribou and you know the birch tree is sacred to the Abnaki. It covers our wigwams, it gives us heat during The Moon Of Snow Blinding and makes our canoes the fastest on the river!"

"But look, Father." Red Feather bent over and picked up a small-blackened birch leaf and held it for his father to see. Then he crushed it in his hand and then opened it to show there was only a small bit of black powder left. Red Feather then blew the black powder off his hand. "See, it goes to nothing. It has no spirit. I do not believe in spirits without eyes and a beating heart."

"You are wrong! The spirit has left but you must still pray for it. When the blood flows red in the Abnaki or the caribou the spirit is there. When the green blood of the leaf flows, its spirit is there. But when the green blood is gone its spirit has left, but you still must pray for the spirit's long life."

Red Feather looked at his father but said nothing. Graywolf was embarrassed for his friend Running Bear and told the group they should head back to the village and tell the others the lost children had been found. The trip home was in solemn silence. Red Feather looked dejected. Running Bear did not know that his son had such radical thoughts about the sacred birch tree and worried that the tribe might shun the boy. Little Turtle wondered how they would ever defeat the giant eel now that Red Feather had denounced three of the Abnaki's most powerful spirits.

Chapter Three

Little Turtle's Long Path

G raywolf breathed the pleasant smell of pine as he crushed the heavy coating of brown needles underfoot on the path to Running Bear's wigwam. He noticed that the trees by the river were almost bare. His damaged right arm dangled uselessly by his side. The flesh wounds had healed but the eel had crushed the bones and they had not set properly. He could not bend his arm at all. Still he wanted to find out how Running Bear's wound was healing. Running Bear's wife, Yellow Bird, greeted him.

"Running Bear is by the river. He spends much time there."

Graywolf walked to the river and saw Running Bear sitting alone.

"How is your leg?"

"It is fully healed and does not bother me. It is my son that disturbs me."

"Oh, you mean the problem at the fire?"

"Yes, I'm concerned that he may not have a long life. I have spoken with him and he does not believe in our most powerful spirits."

"Do not worry, Running Bear. Young braves sometimes challenge their parent's beliefs. He will change when he gets older."

"But he may not live to be older!"

Graywolf thought about how to console Running Bear. "Has Red Feather met with his guardian spirit?"

"Yes, during the past Moon Of Moose Calling."

"What did the spirit say?"

"He was told that he would be a great hunter and warrior."

"Then there is nothing to worry about. He will live to grow old."

Running Bear said nothing.

"Little Turtle must meet his guardian spirit. I have been waiting for my arm to heal. It is hard to have a son live alone in the woods for days without food or water waiting for his guardian spirit, but I must begin before the moon sets tonight."

At that Graywolf left his friend and went back to his wigwam. White Cloud was outside.

"Where is Little Turtle?"

"Probably fishing again above the falls."

Graywolf found his son and Red Feather where White Cloud had said.

"Come Little Turtle, we must prepare a lean-to for you to meet your guardian spirit."

Little Turtle did not argue with his father. He wound in his line and walked with his father back to the village. His mother was preparing the noon meal on a small fire outside. His father went ahead and entered the wigwam.

"Mother, why must I go to meet my guardian spirit? I know that I must be a great warrior and hunter like Graywolf."

White Cloud walked to the nearest birch tree and plucked one of its leaves. She came back to Little Turtle and held the leaf up to the sunlight so Little Turtle could see all the veins in the leaf.

"Every Abnaki has one path to a long life like every leaf has one long vein." aid White Cloud pointing to the long vein running down the center of the leaf. "As you can see the leaf also has many short veins, and there are many short paths that the Abnaki can take, but only one long one. You must council with your guardian spirit to understand what you long path is."

Little Turtle was disappointed that he would have to go through the ordeal of living alone in the woods without food or water until his guardian spirit appeared, but knew every young brave had to do it.

Graywolf came out of the wigwam and motioned for Little Turtle to go with him.

The two walked into the woods for some time before Graywolf stopped and began gathering tree branches and told Little Turtle to do the same. The branches were trimmed and assembled into a crude lean-to.

"You must wait here for your guardian spirit, Little Turtle," Graywolf said as he gave him his last drink of water from a small bark container. "I will return after the spirit has spoken to you."

Graywolf walked away back to the path they had followed into the woods. He turned and waved good-bye. Little Turtle looked at the lean-to and then walked away from it, surveying the forest around it. The place was thick with oak trees, several pines and few birch. The earth was covered with broken branches, brown leaves and pine needles. As the sun went down the forest of dark tree trunks and the mantle of overhead branches crowded in on him and he retreated inside the lean-to. He did not sleep, but listened to the sounds of the night forest, the owl, the wolf and the coyote.

"I hope the spirit comes tonight and then I will return to the wigwam in the morning."

But the spirit did not come. Awakened by the strong morning sun, Little Turtle felt alone and hungry. He busied himself walking the woods close to the lean-to. From his talks with Red Feather the spirit would come at night and he did not want to spend any more time in the lean-to than was necessary. A storm came in the afternoon and he retreated again to the lean-to but found the makeshift roof of tree branches did little to keep the rain out and found a nearby large oak tree that offered as much protection and seemed a more pleasant place to sit. He couldn't avoid getting wet. He spent the afternoon trying to dry his clothes, wringing out his deerskin shirt and leggings one piece at a time. He put them back on hoping his body heat would dry them before nightfall when it would get colder. Now daring to walk further from the lean-to he found a small clearing where he could see the sun go down behind the ridge of western mountains and stayed there to watch the clouds change color from white and gray to streaks of orange. Little Turtle waited as long as he could to return to the lean-to.

The second night was like the first except he was now more tired and hungry.

"I do not think I can wait much longer," Little Turtle thought to himself.

Sleep overtook him quickly that night. He'd wanted desperately to stay awake to not miss his guardian spirit, but he'd covered himself with pine needles and was much warmer than the night before and could not keep his eyes open.

Morning arrived and still no guardian spirit. Little Turtle was till hungry and thirsty. He stood up shaking the pine needles from his clothes and hair and felt the belt holding up his leggings fall to his knees. He pulled them up quickly and retied his belt.

"I can't go through another day of this!" he thought. "I just woke up and I'm still tired. I'm thirsty, hungry and bored! Please come tonight, guardian spirit! I want to go back to the wigwam!"

The birds were announcing the arrival of another day. Little Turtle stretched then walked into the open and decided to count all the birds he could see. They were easy to spot with the leaves off the trees. By noon Little Turtle felt he was too weak to take his daily walks in the woods and sat under the oak tree getting up to take small walks around the lean-to now and then. That afternoon he began hearing strange noises coming from the forest but looked and saw nothing.

At nightfall Little Turtle went to the lean-to. Looking into the darkness he saw visions of rising smoke from the pine needles he had used to cover himself. Fearing fire would soon erupt from the smoke he quickly tried to stamp out the area the smoke was coming from. He looked closely and realized there was no burning at all. Why was he beginning to see things that weren't there?

The strange noises continued from the forest as Little Turtle once again covered his body with pine needles to stay warm, and then drifted in and out of sleep as the strange noises in the forest did not stop.

On the fourth day, Little Turtle was now so weak from lack of food or water that he didn't leave the lean-to at all. At times he simply sat up to shed more of the pine needles as the day warmed. In the sunlight coming through the trees he thought he saw his mother and his sister coming, but when he called to them no one answered.

Trying to stand on several occasions, he felt disoriented and dizzy and would then collapse, upset that he could not understand what was happening to him.

The lack of food and water made his deerskin shirt and leggings hang loosely on his body. Somehow he no longer wished for food. In mid afternoon Little Turtle fell into a stupor and began thrashing about the lean-to fighting monsters that weren't there.

His body finally went limp and stayed motionless until sleep came again.

It had been dark for some time when the smell of a sweet tobacco woke Little Turtle. He thought there was something in the corner of the lean-to. He rubbed his eyes and tried to focus them. There he saw what looked like an old Abnaki with long gray hair, smoking a pipe. He was wearing a headband with no feathers and was covered with a gray blanket. The old man took the pipe from his mouth.

"Little Turtle, I am your guardian spirit. I have come to tell you that your long path is that of a great shaman. Your wisdom will grow and you will bring needed healing to your tribe."

"No!!!" exploded Little Turtle, "I am to be a great warrior and hunter like my father, Graywolf!!!" He kept yelling this over and over as the image of the spirit faded to nothing and he wept himself back to sleep.

As daylight broke the next morning, something wet was being stroked across his forehead. Little Turtle opened his eyes to see Graywolf standing over him. He helped Little Turtle to a sitting position and gave him the birch container of water that he drank from until it was empty.

"Are you alright?"

"Yes, Father."

Little Turtle tried to stand but fell back to a sitting position. Graywolf offered a hand and held him upright waiting for Little Turtle to regain his sense of balance.

"I brought dried fish," Graywolf said as he passed the pouch to Little Turtle.

"I cannot eat, Father. I am not hungry."

"But you must try."

Little Turtle took the pouch back and put a very small piece in his mouth and ate it with difficulty. Graywolf did not press him to eat more. They walked slowly to the path with Graywolf holding his son upright. Both said nothing until Little Turtle seemed steadier on his feet.

"Did you see your guardian spirit?"

"Yes."

"What is your long path?"

There was a long silence. Little Turtle did not want to tell his father but he couldn't lie to him.

"I am to be a shaman, but I want to be a great warrior and hunter like you, Graywolf!"

"That is good, Little Turtle. Manyfeathers is growing old and the tribe will need a new shaman. Is that all he said?"

"No...he said that I am to be a reat shaman."

Graywolf seemed pleased. He felt that his son did not have the skills of a great warrior and this would keep his son from having to go into battle.

Little Turtle was very dejected. He could not tell his father or mother about his pact to kill the giant eel. They would surely not approve. If his sister told anyone about the pact, Red Feather would not help him attack the eel and Red Feather had offended all the great spirits that could help with the attack. And now his long path was to be that of the shaman! "How will ever be able to slay the giant eel?" The more he thought about the problems, the more despondent he became. He did not even return his mother's greeting when he approached the wigwam. He simply went into the wigwam and sulked in the darkness.

"He'll be alright, White Cloud...just very tired. The spirit was good to our son. He is to be a great shaman!"

White Cloud smiled.

Little Turtle was unsure what to do next. His plans now seemed out of reach. How could he change his guardian spirit's message? There was really no one he could talk to.

" nnot tell mother or father. They are happy I am to become a shaman. The only two I can talk to are Twilight and Red Feather and surely they cannot change my long path!"

Then Manyfeathers came to mind. He had cured Twilight's fever and Graywolf had sought his advice many times. And Manyfeathers was a shaman. Perhaps he had the power to change Little Turtle's long path!

Approaching Manyfeathers wigwam in a hurry, he hardly noticed the colorful pictures of eagles on the skins covering it.

Quickly opening the flap he rushed inside almost bumping into Manyfeathers who was just starting a fire.

"Why such a hurry, young brave? Is your wigwam on fire?"

"No Manyfeathers, but I have many problems to talk about!"

"Everyone who comes here has problems young one. Someday perhaps someone will enter my wigwam without a problem!"

"Yes Manyfeathers, but will you promise not to tell anyone else about my problems? Not even my father, Graywolf or my mother?"

"If it does them no harm then I will not tell."

Little Turtle told Manyfeathers about his secret pact with Red Feather to kill the Mohawk eel.

"But my guardian spirit has told me that I am to be a shaman and not the great warrior that I want to be. You must change my long path! And my friend Red Feather thinks we cannot kill the eel and he laughs at the Spirit Of The Waters, The Spirit Of The Wind and The Spirit Of The Birch Tree. We will no longer have their help! Even though he taunts the spirits nothing ever happens to him. I no longer know what to believe!"

"You have so many big problems for such a small boy! I don't know where to start!"

Manyfeathers sat in the corner puffing on his pipe for such a long time. Little Turtle noticed the large eagle, Yellow Beak, staring down at him from his perch at the top of the wigwam. Manyfeathers put down his pipe.

"Your guardian spirit has spoken. I cannot change your long path. Yellowbeak and I will teach you well the ways of the shaman, for the eagle is wiser than I am.

A new shaman will be needed, Little Turtle, for I am getting too old."

Manyfeathers looked at the boy and saw the dejected look on his face. He decided to say no more about becoming a shaman and went on to Little Turtle's other problems.

"We live in a spirit world. Without The Spirit Of The Waters there are no rivers for the Abnaki to fish. Without the Spirit Of The Forest there is no home for the bear, nowhere for the Abnaki to hunt. Without the Spirit Of The Wind the eagle cannot fly, there is no rain and the plantings will not grow. Your friend must understand this. And you must remember that it will not be your guardian spirit or Manyfeathers or Graywolf that decides what path you take."

Then he reached into his stack of kindling wood and took a small stick and poked Little Turtle in the belly with it. "Whenever you have a big problem there are two wolves fighting in here. Today it is the wolf of the shaman fighting the warrior wolf. Tomorrow the wolves will be different."

"But Manyfeathers, which wolf will win?"

"That is what you must understand. It will always be the wolf you feed."

Little Turtle looked puzzled for a moment and then a smile came to his face. Manyfeathers reached up and Yellowbeak jumped onto his arm. He pushed aside the deerskin flap and the eagle flew away.

"To understand why your friend is not punished when he laughs at the spirits without eyes and a beating heart, you need to understand the tree. When the Moon Of Snow Blinding comes, the bare tree will live, but it cannot grow until the leaf returns. If the tree does not grow with the rest of the forest, it will stay small. It will not see the sun, only darkness. Like a tree without the leaf, the brave who does not believe in the spirits can live but cannot grow."

There was a flutter of wings outside the wigwam and Manyfeathers again pushed aside the deerskin flap. The eagle flew to his perch holding a small green birch leaf.

Manyfeathers took the leaf and tucked it into Little Turtles headband.

"Yellowbeak gives this to remind you that as long as you feed the wolf that believes in the spirits, your leaf will be forever green."

Little Turtle paused for a moment to think about what Manyfeathers said. He thanked them and left. On his return to Graywolf's wigwam he noticed that the trees were bare and the leaves on the ground had all turned brown.

"Where did Yellowbeak find a green leaf?"

As he walked the path the Abnaki drums were still beating out the message that Little Turtle was to become a great shaman! Drums that were heard all the way down the Ashweelot River to the territory of their bitter enemies, the Mohawks!

Chapter Four

Mystery and a Mohawk Plot

Little Turtle could hardly contain his excitement after the meeting with Manyfeathers. He rushed to the river and found Red Feather still fishing.

"I have great news!" he yelled to his friend. "I must talk to you!"

Red Feather reluctantly left his fishing rock and came to shore.

"What is it?"

"I must feed the warrior wolf and you must feed the wolf that believes in spirits without eyes and a beating heart!"

"What are you talking about?"

Little Turtle told what happened when he talked to Manyfeathers. "I will be a great warrior if I feed the warrior wolf in here!" Little Turtle said pointing to his stomach. "And you must feed the wolf that believes in the spirits without eyes or you will live in darkness."

"Little Turtle, what you eat cannot help you come like the fox, attack like the lion and leave like the bird! And what I eat will not make me live in darkness"

"No, Red Feather, it is not about what we eat but what we believe!"

"Then that's what you should say! Your words sound like the shaman's, not the words of a warrior! And I do not believe in spirits without eyes and a beating heart and I do not live in darkness"

"But you will Red Feather because you will not grow!"

"I do not know what you are talking about. Why do you wear that leaf?"

"It is a gift from Yellowbeak. If I believe in the spirits the leaf will be forever green."

"You are foolish, Little Turtle. Leaves do not stay green. They turn brown and fall from the tree. There is no spirit!"

Little Turtle thought for a moment. How could he get his friend to believe in the spirits without eyes? "Come, we will take a walk above the planting fields." As they walked Little Turtle asked, "Do you remember when the tribe rushed to put out the fire above our planting fields?"

"Yes," Red Feather answered. "Like the birch tree, the grasses were all black and dead."

As the two entered the burned area, Little Turtle stopped his friend. "Would you say that this is dead, black grass that you can crush in your hand and blow away as you did the birch leaf?"

"Yes," Red Feather replied.

Little Turtle knelt down closer to the burned grass and asked his friend to do the same. "Look closely, is it really just dead grass as you say?"

He peered into the black patch and there were little shoots of green grass growing between the blackened ones. Red Feather scratched his head. "That's strange. I thought the grass was all dead."

"Things are not always as they seem, Red Feather. The grass is really not dead. The spirit only left and is now returning. The spirit will return to the blackened birch, just as the leaf returns to all the trees after the Moon Of Snow Blinding."

Red Feather looked puzzled, but he was not ready to agree with Little Turtle.

Meanwhile, Graywolf walked the path again to Running Bear's wigwam. He wanted to see if his friend's leg wound had healed. Otter Tail had seen a family of wild boar near a ravine north of the village but he did not want to hunt the boar without Running Bear who was the tribe's best hunter. He also thought about taking Little Turtle on the hunt. He was now old enough and the excitement might take his mind off the disappointment with his guardian spirit's message.

"Running Bear, Otter Tail has seen the wild boar near the ravine north of the planting fields. Are you well enough to hunt? I would like to take my son with us."

"Yes, the wound is healed. If you take Little Turtle, Red Feather will be disappointed if he must stay home."

"Then both should go. They must be fishing. Let us go to the river."

The smell of pine was everywhere as they walked the trail to the river. Little Turtle looked up as Graywolf and Running Bear came down the riverbank.

"We cannot talk about my meeting with Manyfeathers!" Little Turtle said to his friend as they watched their fathers approach.

"We want to talk to you," Graywolf explained. "Early tomorrow we will be taking a hunting party north to catch the wild boar. Running Bear and I have agreed that both of you can come."

The two boys looked at each other with smiles on their faces.

"Have you been on a hunt, Red Feather?"

"No"

"I have not!" exclaimed an excited Little Turtle.

"You must go to sleep early tonight, young braves. We will have to leave in darkness to reach the ridge and return before dark," Running Bear said looking at both boys. All four returned to the village together.

White Cloud was puzzled by the sudden excitement on her son's face. "What have you promised the boy now, Graywolf?" she asked.

"We are going to take Little Turtle and Running Bear's son on their first hunt tomorrow." Graywolf noticed the disappointment on Twilight's face. "I'm sorry, Twilight, but you are too young.

Little Turtle and his father busied themselves gathering their best arrows and checking the condition of their longbows before they bedded down for the night.

Graywolf shook Little Turtle's shoulder in the darkness. The two dressed and left the wigwam without waking White Cloud or Twilight. They walked the path to the north edge of the village where they met Otter Tail, Broken Bow, Running Bear, Red Feather and several other braves. All the braves had longbows and several carried small drums. Graywolf led the group further north past the planting fields in the moonlight. The cold night air gave way to bright sunlight, a cloudless sky and a warm wind. The trail ahead of them was thick with trees. It twisted and turned along the bank of a shallow stream rising gently until reaching a broad clearing at the foothills of the mountains. At the far edge of the clearing was a cliff. The Abnaki would often try to trap caribou and deer against it. The clearing was covered with tall grasses, low bushes and a few small trees.

To trap game, two rows of braves with longbows would form walls coming out from the ravine about twice the range of the longbow apart. A third line of braves would form some distance away and move towards the ravine to join with the longbows and trap the game against the cliff.

Running Bear positioned the two lines of longbows and returned to the group.

"Otter Tail, you will anchor the left side of the moving line. Little Turtle will be with you. Running Bear will be on the right end. His son will be with him. I will lead the line from the center where the boar will likely attack," Graywolf explained.

Graywolf formed the wall of braves and held the longbow high over his head as a signal for the line to start moving towards the ravine. The line of braves began to beat the small drums and yell loudly as they moved to close with the bowmen. They had moved a short distance when there was movement in the thick grass ahead of them.

The large black head of a boar would appear and then disappear in the bushes ahead of them darting first this way then that, but always moving away from the yelling and loud drumbeats and towards the cliff. As the line moved steadily towards the ravine the boar's flight quickened. Snorting and hoof beats were now intermingled with the sound of drums as the moving line closed with the bowmen. The braves raised their longbows! The boar darted back and forth along the edge of the ravine, its black hulk now clearly visible. As the arrows flew the boar tried to bolt Graywolf's line. Not in the middle but the left side, right at Little Turtle! Otter Tail saw the beast charging and jumped to get in front of Little

Turtle but his foot got caught in the roots of a low bush and he fell. He looked up to see Little Turtle's body being thrown into the air believing the boar had run through him. He ran to the body. Little Turtle was sitting there dazed and covered with dirt while the rest of the braves chased after the boar.

"Are you hurt?"

"I don't think so," Little Turtle said moving his body this way and that.

"Where did the boar hit you?"

"I didn't feel anything," Little Turtle replied.

"The boar must have hit you. I saw you flying through the air!"

"I didn't feel anything! I saw the boar coming at me and I was numb with fear. Then I saw it pass under me! That's all I remember."

Otter Tail scratched his head not knowing what to think or tell his father. Aside from being dirty, Little Turtle seemed fine. Otter Tail then breathed a sigh of relief. He had been in charge of his chief's son. Then Otter Tail spotted a small green birch leaf beside Little Turtle and reached down to pick it up, but Little Turtle picked it up first and tucked it back into his headband.

"That's mine! It's a gift from Yellowbeak."

Graywolf approached, "Is Little Turtle alright?"

"I'm fine, Father." Little Turtle answered standing and brushing off the dirt.

Red Feather and Running Bear came back with the rest of the braves. The wild boar had escaped.

"We cannot catch him now. We will return another day," Graywolf said. The group started back to their home, disappointed they had come so close to getting the boar and now had the long walk home ahead of them without anything to show for their efforts.

Some distance from the mouth of the Ashweelot, a Mohawk brave fishing in the river heard the drums beating out the message that the spirits had given the Abnakis a great shaman.

"I must tell Thunder Cloud," he thought as he pulled in his line and began paddling quickly back to camp.

He pulled the dugout on shore and rushed to his chief's wigwam.

"The Abnakis now have a powerful new shaman!"

Chief Thunder Cloud was sitting before a meal of corn and turkey stew while his wife was still cooking outside.

"Bring Black Dog here." He said to the brave. "He will not be happy to hear this!"

Black Dog, the Mohawk shaman, entered his chief's wigwam and Thunder Cloud told him the Abnakis had been given a great shaman.

Black Dog slammed the clay pot he was carrying on the wigwam floor breaking it into many pieces that flew across the wigwam. One of the pieces plopped into Thunderclouds stew. Black Dog could see the angry look on his chief's face as he threw the wet piece of clay out of the wigwam.

"You must control your temper, Black Dog! You anger too easily!"

"But we cannot allow the Abnaki shaman to live. There cannot be a greater shaman on the river than Black Dog! If he is a greater shaman he will take command of the giant eel. It has taken a long time to get control of the eel. The Abnakis can outrun our dugouts but they cannot outrun the eel. That is why Graywolf has not come back to attack the Mohawks. He knows this! If the Abnakis control the eel they will again command the river and we will be at their mercy!"

"You are right, Black Dog. I will call a war council." Chief Thundercloud assembled his braves and spoke to them. "The Abnakis have a young brave named Little Turtle who is to become a great shaman. He cannot be allowed to live and take command of the giant eel. I want Beaver Paw, Flying Wing and Sitting Deer to scout their village."

An older Mohawk brave named Two Arrows stepped forward. "I have traded skins with the Pequot many times. We do not trade with the Abnaki now but they do. I will take more skins to trade with the Pequot and find out about this young brave called Little Turtle."

"Good! I do not want to further anger the Abnaki chief Graywolf. He has not sought revenge, perhaps because of the eel. But they are fierce warriors when he leads them. Our plan must insure that Graywolf does not know that the Mohawks killed their young shaman."

Two Arrows loaded a dugout with furs and skins the next morning and headed south down the Connecticut River to the Pequot camp. The three scouts then prepared another dugout and waited until darkness came before going north on the Ashweelot.

After several hours paddling against the current the three Mohawks noticed an orange light above the horizon further north. Soon they could hear the roar of Great Falls in the distance. Rounding a large bend in the river they could see Abnaki braves at the base of the falls carrying lighted torches. The light from the torches lit up the river.

"We cannot go further, or we will be seen by the Abnaki " Beaver Paw said. The group pulled their dugout into shore. "The riverbank is very steep. Be careful not to move rocks with your feet. They will fall into the river and we will be heard!"

They climbed the bank and moved through the trees close to the path leading to the Abnaki village. When the Mohawks came to the camp there was light from two fires and the three stayed in the trees counting wigwams and then made their way to the river to observe the canoes the Abnacki had. They moved back towards their dugouts on the ridge above the salmon fishermen and stopped before descending the steep bank.

"It will be difficult to attack the Abnaki at night. We must make sure we are not seen on the way up the riverbank with so many braves. Let us descend the riverbank further south where there are more trees."

The three Mohawk braves scouted a way up and down the riverbank that a large group of braves could take and not be seen from the base of the falls. They pushed their dugout quietly into the dark river and let the current carry them south until they were sure the noise of their paddling could not be heard.

After beaching the dugout at their camp the three went straight to Thundercloud's wigwam.

"The Abnaki tribe is much smaller than the Mohawk but their village is difficult to attack. The village is high above the Ashweelot falling waters with steep banks to climb from the river. They fish below the falls with torches and we would have to leave our canoes a long way down river if we are not to be seen. They have many birch canoes and seven war dugouts," Beaver Paw told his chief.

"We will wait for news from Two Arrows," Thundercloud answered.

It was three more days before Two Arrows returned. Thundercloud summoned Black Dog and the three scouts.

"I have spoken with the Pequot," Two Arrows began. "Little Turtle is the son of Graywolf and is a very young brave. Graywolf told them that his son often brings home fish for their family but they argue that he doesn't do his morning work because he leaves the wigwam in the dark to go fishing."

Then Thundercloud spoke, "We cannot attack the village, Graywolf would know that the Mohawks killed his son. That must not happen. Black Dog, you are the most cunning among us. How can we kill Little Turtle and have Graywolf believe it was an accident."

"We are a much bigger tribe than the Abnaki. We should destroy their village! Then there will be no more trouble. The great shaman will be no more! Why are you afraid of an Abnaki with one arm?" Black Dog yelled angrily.

"Calm yourself, Black Dog! Go back to your wigwam and devise a plan to do as I have asked! I am chief and will not slaughter the Abnaki and the Mohawks because you say to!"

Black Dog returned to his wigwam unhappy over his leader's decision not to attack the village. He sulked in the darkness thinking about how to rid the threat of the new Abnaki shaman without attacking their village until he fell asleep.

Chapter Five

Black Dogs Victory

Black Dog awoke the next morning with the sun coming through the entrance of his wigwam and lighting the dirt floor. Angrily, he took the point of his long spear and scratched the name Little Turtle in the dirt. Over and over he would write the name then stamp it out violently with his feet, spinning round and round until the name was gone. Black Dog did this several times until he fell exhausted onto the floor.

"I will find a way to destroy the great Abnaki shaman if I have to do it myself!" Then a cunning, evil thought came to his head. His anger faded suddenly and a smile stretched across his face form ear to ear. "I know how! I will command the eel to do it! I have the plan!!!"

Black Dog went quickly to his chief's wigwam.

"I have a way to rid ourselves of this great Abnaki shaman! Little Turtle is a fisherman. I will command the eel to do it!!!"

Thundercloud was not impressed. "Did you forget that the Abnaki fish at night with torches and spears? The torches are for attracting the fish but they also light the water! Everyone there will see the eel! They will know that the Mohawks killed him!!"

"But wait, Thundercloud! We don't know that Little Turtle fishes below the falls where it is lighted by the torches! Two Arrows said he fishes in the morning darkness!"

"And what if he fishes above the falls? How will you get the eel there?"

"We would take him upriver at night in a war dugout and carry him to the place above the falls. The eel would strike in the morning darkness and Graywolf would not know."

"We must be certain where the boy fishes."

Thundercloud met again with Beaver Paw, Flying Wing and Sitting Deer. They returned to the Abnaki territory that night, climbing the steep riverbank out of the light coming from the torches at base of the falls. From the riverbank above where the Abnakis were salmon fishing they saw that there were no boys in the group. That night they stayed above the falls near the trail from the village and waited for Little Turtle to go fishing.

"Hurry Little Turtle, it will be light soon." Red Feather said anxiously as the boys walked quickly down the path past the three Mohawks hiding in the trees.

They watched the two boys bait their hooks and move out onto the rocks in the river above the falls. It was beginning to get light. The Mohawk braves moved quietly back to their dugout and down the Ashweelot. They reported to Thundercloud and Black Dog that Little Turtle fished with a friend above the falls.

"Good!" offered Black Dog, "On the next night of the covered moon we will put the eel in the river where they fish. The eel will take care of both of them!"

Two days later a dense evening fog turned into a dreary night. Dark rain clouds covered the moonless sky as Black dog and the three Mohawk scouts prepared the dugout for the trip up the Ashweelot. They carried torches for light as Black Dog approached the river with the three scouts and called to the eel. The eel made strange screeching noises as it swam to shore. Beaver Paw wrapped a deerskin around the eel's large snout while Flying Wing tied it with long pieces of root so it could not bite them. It took all four of them to load the giant eel onto the war dugout. Even though they had taken the tribes largest war canoe the head of the eel stuck out over the front and it's tail dragged in the water behind!

The trip was so dark and dismal that the torches had to be used to find their way up river. When they approached Abnaki territory there was no orange light in the sky, only the roar of the falls.

"We are in luck!" Bear Paw said to the others. "The night is not fit for Abnaki fishing!"

The dugout was able to carry the eel all the way to the base of the falls, but there the torches had to be put out. They dare not use them this close to the Abnaki village. With Black Dog in the lead the four braves hoisted the eel onto their shoulders in the darkness and struggled up the steep riverbank. The eel was very heavy and they stopped to rest several times before reaching the top.

"Take the trail north," Flying Wing told Black Dog. "It is not far."

The group had difficulty staying on the trail. Occasionally, a glimmer of light from the river would let them see where they were going.

"This is where they were fishing," Sitting Deer said.

The group put down the eel. Beaver Paw untied the skin covering its snout and they watched the huge eel slither down the bank and into the river.

"I have told the eel what to do!" said Black Dog with a cunning smile on his face.

They returned to the Mohawk camp and Black Dog told Thundercloud they no longer had to worry about the Abnaki's great shaman!

The boys fished the river above the falls from early the following morning until the sun was well above the mountains, but no fish were caught. The river had fallen during The Moon Of Moose Calling and the water was now too shallow near the rocks they stood on.

"We will have to use the canoe tomorrow to get to deeper water, Little Turtle. The fishing will be better out on the river."

Little Turtle nodded in agreement. They headed back towards the village and stopped to check the canoe they would use the next morning. As the two inspected the canoe for leaks, Red Feather noticed that his friend still had the little birch leaf tucked in his headband.

"Why do you still wear that silly leaf?"

"It is not silly!" said Little Turtle pulling the leaf out to look at. "It is a gift from Yellowbeak. And look, it is still green! Do you see any other leaf that is still green?"

"No, but it is just a leaf even if it is green!"

"You are wrong, Red Feather. It is a special leaf. I wore it on the hunt and something lifted me so the boar didn't kill me."

"The boar just missed you, that's all!"

"Then why does the leaf stay green?"

Red Feather s voice turned angry, "I do not know but it is just a common leaf. It is not a magic leaf!"

They left the riverfront and returned to the village without another word. Red eather thought about how much arguing they were doing over such an ordinary thing as a leaf.

"First there was the problem with my father and the burned birch leaf. Now my best friend thinks he has a magic leaf. He probably thinks he's invincible just because he has a leaf!" Red Feather thought to himself.

"I'll be here early, Little Turtle. It will take a while to get the canoe out on the river."

Little Turtle grunted in agreement as he walked past his mother grinding corn outside his wigwam.

"Your father has gone hunting and I have work for you, Little Turtle. You can finish grinding the corn or go back to the river for water."

"I'll get the water," Little Turtle replied heading to the river with a birch bark container in each hand. Then he and Twilight helped stretch a new deerskin that his mother had scrapped clean of hair. After the evening meal he and his sister went into the woods to find firewood. That evening, sitting around the fire in the middle of the wigwam they listened to one of Graywolf's many stories about how the spirits had befriended him and other Abnakis when he was a young brave. Then White Cloud told them it was time for bed.

The fire went out and it grew colder. Little Turtle could not sleep. He couldn't help think about his argument with Red Feather that day. Moonlight came through the opening at the top of the wigwam and cast a circle of light on the floor next to Little Turtle. He remembered the circle of sunlight coming down from the top of Manyfeathers wigwam. His hand fumbled in the darkness until he felt his headband. He pulled the birch leaf from it and put in the small circle of light.

Then Little Turtle whispered softly as if talking to the leaf, "I must avenge the Mohawk attack! Red Feather believes we cannot succeed, but he has made a promise that cannot be broken! I will only feed the wolf that believes we can! Red Feather does not believe in spirits without eyes or a beating heart. But Manyfeathers is right. Without the mountains to catch the snow there are no rivers. Without the rivers there are no fish for the Abnaki. Without the wind to bring the rain there is no forest to hunt the caribou, no crops to harvest. If there were no spirits *without* eyes then there would be no spirits *with* eyes! It is true what Manyfeathers has said. The Abnakis are only small spirits among many powerful spirits. I must respect them!"

Then Little Turtle picked up the leaf and held it up for the moonlight to shine through as White Cloud had done to show him the many veins in a leaf, but no light came through.

"Why do you have no paths, little leaf? Why do you stay green? Did you save me from wild boar? Are you a magic leaf?"

Little Turtle stared at the leaf in his hand until his eyelids became heavy and he fell asleep.

"Who...who," came the cry of the owl again from right outside his wigwam. Little Turtle stirred from under his bearskin blanket. The second time the owl cried he awoke and dressed quickly, gathering his fishing gear as he moved to the door of the wigwam. Little Turtle started south down the riverbank trail.

"Where are you going?" Red Feather asked.

"Fishing," was the sleepy reply.

"Have you forgotten that we are fishing from the canoe?"

"Oh...I remember now," Little Turtle replied.

The two boys headed towards the canoes at the village waterfront. Red Feather went to the back of the canoe while his friend steadied the front of it. Little Turtle got in front while Red Feather steadied the canoe with his paddle thrust into the sand below the shallow water. Then both pushed off onto the river. There was hardly any light to see by that morning.

"We will have to listen carefully to the noise of the falls, it will be difficult to see how close we are to it " Little Turtle offered.

They paddled until they felt the swift current in the middle quicken the speed of their canoe downstream and then backed just out of the current. Now they were drifting slowly towards the falls. Both put their paddles in the canoe and threw out fishing lines. Over and over the two would drift towards the falls while fishing and then the roar of the falls would tell them they it was time to paddle away from it again.

After drifting and fishing then paddling back up-river in the darkness several times, Red Feather yelled in a frightened voice, "Quick! Head to shore!"

"What is it?" Little Turtle wanted to know as they paddled frantically towards shore.

"I felt something with my paddle! It wasn't a fish. It was big!"

They pulled the canoe on shore and sat on an old log on the beach.

"It could have been a log. I have seen logs underwater being carried to the falls " Little Turtle offered.

"It wasn't a log. It was alive!"

"Red Feather, if we wait until it is light the fishing will not be as good. You said this yourself!"

"Why are you now so brave, Little Turtle? I know it's because of that stupid leaf! Do you still have it with you?"

"Yes! It is not a stupid leaf. It is a gift from Yellow-beak. You should show the shaman's eagle respect! Why are you so afraid? You tell me your long path is that of the warrior!"

"Alright, we'll go back out and fish but there is something out there and it is not a dead tree!"

The canoe left shore with the boys still arguing. Light was beginning to fill the sky in the east and the noise of waking birds could be heard from the trees on shore. The light was enough to see the ripples in the water and they could tell where the swift current began. Instead of fishing the two boys kept arguing. Red Feather was especially upset because his friend had questioned his bravery...something Little Turtle had never done before.

"Why do you think I am not a warrior? Does a warrior fight a battle he cannot win? It is the leaf that makes you believe such a foolish thing!"

At that point Red Feather became so angry that he grabbed the leaf from Little Turtles headband and threw it into the river! Now Little Turtle became angry and the two boys began to fight with each other, almost tipping the canoe over. They struggled until one of them noticed large ripples in the water circling the canoe. he ripples ein made by a large glowing green object were circling the canoe. The arguing had caused them to forget they were drifting dangerously close to the falls! Suddenly the huge tail of the beast circling the canoe came out of the water, raised itself high above the canoe and came crashing down on them, cutting the canoe in half! Then pieces of the canoe and the bodies of the two boys disappeared over the edge of the falls!!!

When the boys did not return that afternoon, Graywolf and Running Bear formed a search party to look for them. The fishing spot on the rocks above the falls showed no evidence that the two boys had been there. Then it was discovered that one of the birch canoes was missing. The search party split up with one group looking along the village shore while the other group paddled across the river to search the other side. There was no sign of the boys and without words they descended the steep riverbank dreading what they might find below the falls.

"Look there!" Running Bear shouted above the roar of the falls and pointing to the rocks on the other side across the foaming water. It looked like pieces of one of their canoes! They searched both side of the river below the falls but all they ever found was a small part of canoe the boys must have used. The boys and the rest of the canoe must have been swept downriver!

The tribe mourned the loss of the two young braves all through the Moon Of Snow Blinding. Braves, who fished through the ice in the evening, swore they could hear the voices of the boys. Others complained that visions of the two kept them from sleeping. It was normally a period when a lot of time was spent inside the wigwam playing games, but the young braves now complained that the spirits of the two boys were interrupting their play. Strange markings appeared in the dirt floor of Manyfeathers wigwam that even he could not explain. Graywolf and Running Bear looked at the markings but could not make sense of them.

"We must move our village!" Broken Bow said to White Cloud and Graywolf. A large group of the tribe had gathered outside Graywolf's wigwam. "No one is sleeping. The young braves are afraid to fish the river and even to stay in the wigwam at night! The spirits of Little Turtle and Red Feather will always be here, so we must move!"

Graywolf looked at White Cloud and saw that she w   very tired. He knew what Broken Bow said was true and counseled with the rest of the tribe. The tribe decided to move further north on the river. When the Moon Of Leaf Opening arrived, Graywolf took a large party of braves north to clear an area for their new home. They waited until the ice stopped flowing in the river and then the braves loaded the canoes for the move up river, while the squaws and the older men dragged their belongings north on gatherings of young saplings to the new home.

All that remained at the old village site were the skeletons of wigwams. In time they withered in the wind, rain and snow and fell to the ground. The planting field became overgrown with shrubs and young trees. It was now as if no one had ever lived there except for the howling of the wind at night that sounded like two young Abnaki braves arguing with each other.

Chapter Six

The New Town

M any years went by before anyone came to the old
Abnaki campsite. The first of the new people to
arrive was a man by the name of John Henry Wiggins,
who had spent his working years as the captain of a
big ocean liner that took passengers and cargo to and
from China. John Henry had recently retired to a home
in Neu Boston with his wife, Edna May, ne r where
he grew up, close to the Connecticut river. It was not
long before he became bored. He missed the excitement of commanding a ship and purchased an old
wooden, coal burning, steam driven, paddle wheel
tourist boat, which he named the Edna May. He and
Edna would take trips all alone down the Connecticut
to the seashore and back again but somehow that was
not exciting enough for the old sea captain.

Then one day, Edna May knowing her husband was
still bored had an idea. "Why don't we go upriver and
see what's there?"

John Henry quickly turned the boat around and
headed up the Connecticut studying his maps of the
area as Edna May held the wheel. As the old paddle
wheeler steamed north of Neu Boston they passed only

three farms on the river. Soon there were no more farmers' fields, only rocks and trees. On reaching the mouth of the Ashweelot River they felt alone in the wilderness and decided it would be exciting to explore the new river. They had traveled a long way upriver when Mrs. Wiggins heard something.

"Hear that, Henry?"

"Hear what?"

"There's something ahead!"

"Don't hear a thing, Edna."

It was hard for John Henry to hear her over the noise of the steam engine and the splashing of the paddle wheels.

"Don't know how you ever captained a big ocean liner if you can't hear that!" Edna May snapped.

The noise grew louder and when the Edna May puffed its way around the bend they were staring at a waterfall towering above them, dumping huge amounts of water onto the rocks below. As the boat moved forward the mist from the splashing water was so heavy Captain Wiggins could barely see to drive the boat. Edna May held tightly to the railing as the boat bobbed up and down like a cork in the waves from the falling water. Then the steam engine sputtered and died! John Henry breathed a sigh of relief when the waves pushed the boat into shore without hitting any of the big rocks. Captain Wiggins tied the boat to a tree on shore and started to dry off the engine.

"Don't worry Edna May, I'll have this old engine purring again in no time!"

"John Henry, It's so beautiful here. Why don't we spend the night here on the boat?"

The Captain slowed down drying off the engine while Edna May prepared supper. Afterwards Edna May said, "I'll bet people would pay good money to see this!" pointing to the falls.

The two of them planned late into the night. John Henry would put an advertisement in the Neu Boston

News paper, and have a sign made for the dock where they moored the Edna May. Mrs. Wiggins would buy enough food, drinks, raincoats and umbrellas for the passengers and they would be in business! Both John Henry and Edna May were very excited about their new venture when they arrived back at the dock in Neu Boston. It wasn't long before they were carrying passengers, mostly farmers, up the Ashweelot on Sunday afternoons to look at Great Falls. Edna May made box lunches, but some people got sick bobbing up and down in the boat while they ate. John Henry and Edna May decided to dock the boat so lunch could be eaten either on the boat or on shore. Some people of course would finish eating before the others and would take off up the riverbank just to see what was up there.

"Looks like good farm land," was a comment heard over and over again.

Soon John Henry had to extend the stay on shore so that some of the farmers and their wives could explore above the falls. Their trips upriver became so popular they had to schedule trips on Saturdays to satisfy all the people who wanted to go. Some of the more adventurous farmers and their wives now wanted to build farms on the high ground just above the falls, right where the old Abnaki campsite used to be! It wasn't long before the Edna May was hauling building supplies up river during the week. Several farmers were now clearing trees and rocks and building houses and barns. The rocks made boundary walls for their fields. Between hauling building supplies, food and passengers, John Henry soon had a full time job again! Sometimes the captain and Edna May were so tired after making a trip, they would simply moor their paddle wheeler below the falls and sleep on the boat. John Henry and Edna May were often invited to the farmer's homes and they would climb the steep bank and go there for supper. One time Edna May remarked, "It's so pretty by the river!"

As more farmers began living there, it became impossible for the captain's paddle wheeler to haul all the food and supplies needed. Besides, both John Henry and Edna May were very tired. A farmer turned businessman, named Sandy Simpson, and his two sons built a general store close to the river above the falls. Then a farmer named Cyrus Phineas had someone from Neu Boston build a gristmill on the river to grind the farmers' grain.

Their wives often wanted to shop in Neu Boston where they could buy a lot of things you couldn't find in Simpson's General Store. The farmers held a meeting and decided to widen the old Abnacki trail south all the way to the Connecticut River. That took almost two years and when it was done they decided to build a wooden bridge over the Connecticut to a north-south trail on the other side of the river. Horse drawn carriages loaded with supplies from Neu Boston were soon making their way across the bridge and up the old trail to the new village. It was then that John Henry decided to sell his paddle wheeler and retire for a second time. At first Mrs. Wiggins missed the adventure of traveling to the falls and all the people she had come to know.

"John Henry, why don't we build a house above the falls? The river there is so pretty!"

"But I'm a ship's captain. I don't know how to build a house."

"But the farmers do it " Edna May replied.

John Henry reluctantly sought out a house builder in Neu Boston but found they were all very busy. He put an ad in the Neu Boston News and next day a man showed up at his door.

"Hello, I'm Louie Lamier the builder."

The captain looked at the short, dark haired man standing in his doorway. "There is something different about him," he thought. Then it came to him. Louie had only one eye that moved. The other always stared straight ahead. "Must be a glass eye," John Henry thought to himself again.

"I build houses, Mr. Wiggins. Do you have land on which to build?"

"Yes, but I want it built further north, in the new town called Marlowe. Come in I'll show you on the map and tell you what I want built."

The two men talked for over an hour with Mrs. Wiggins coming in from the kitchen from time to time when she overheard something she wanted to change or make clear. Louie and John Henry shook hands and Louie went off to order supplies and have them hauled to the home site above Great Falls.

The land from the rivers edge sloped upwards and the captain had the house put well above the water so Mrs. Wiggins got a wonderful view of the wide river above the falls. It was a grand house built of wood with many windows facing the water. On one side was a round wooden turret shaped like so many of the stone castles Mrs. Wiggins had seen on her trip to Europe. Mr. Wiggins insisted on a widow's walk on top of the turret, like the old sea captains houses he was familiar with, but Mrs. Wiggins wasn't happy about it.

"This is a river, not the sea. And besides, you are no longer a sea captain. There's no reason for a widow's walk!" Edna May thought it was bad luck to have a widow's walk on her house.

"I'll never use it! Besides it's bad luck!"

"Don't care! A sea captain's house must have a widow's walk!"

Mrs. Wiggins simply walked away. Months later Louie finished the house. Mrs. Wiggins came and walked round and round the house several times.

"There's something strange about this house," she said. "I know. It's not straight. It's crooked!"

Now John Henry had noticed the same thing as he watched Louie build the house, but tried to convince himself and Mrs. Wiggins it was straight.

"I think it's sort of an optical illusion, Edna May."

But Edna May would have none of that. While the arguing continued Louie stood there tilting his head from side to side saying, "It's straight. It's straight."

The captain could see that Edna May was getting very angry. He pulled her away so Louie couldn't hear.

"Look Edna May, the man has a glass eye. Maybe he can't build a straight house."

"You hired a builder who can't build a straight house?"

John Henry didn't answer. He walked to Louie and handed him the last payment. But Edna May was never happy. She just sat looking out one of the windows facing the water, refusing to talk to John Henry.

He would tell her over and over, "If you're bored why don't you invite some of your old friends from Neu Boston?"

"I can't have my friends see that I live in a crooked house!" was the reply she gave the captain each time.

One day Mrs. Wiggins was looking out her window and heard noises next door. She saw Louie digging.

"What are you doing?" she asked

"I'm building another house." Louie replied.

"Whom are you building it for?"

"A Mr. Tuttle from Neu Boston," Louie answered.

Mrs. Wiggins rushed to Neu Boston to find Mr. Tuttle who ran a livery stable business.

"Is Louie Lamier building a house for you?" Edna May asked.

"Yes," Mr. Tuttle replied

"Well Louie built my house and it's crooked!"

Mr. Tuttle returned with Mrs. Wiggins and stood on her front lawn and looked at her house. Like

Louie and Mr. Wiggins, Mr. Tuttle kept tilting his head back and forth and was unsure the house was really crooked.

"It doesn't look that bad, Mrs. Wiggins. Besides, if I build a straight house next to yours, my house would look odd."

Mrs. Wiggins went into the house slamming the door behind her and started to cry.

"I not only have to live in a crooked house, now I'm going to have another one next door!"

John Henry and Edna May argued all the time about the house but John Henry would not move back to Neu Boston.

"Edna May, we just moved here! I've spent our savings on this house because you wanted to live here. Now you tell everyone we own a crooked house. Who do you think will buy it? Besides I'm tired of moving!"

But all that did was make Edna May cry again. John Henry looked outside. It was already dark. e simply had to get away from the arguing and crying! He went down to his dock and took a small rowboat out on the river in the dark. He never returned. His rowboat was found across the river smashed into small pieces. From time to time there had been stories about a snakelike monster that lived in the river but no one could really explain what had happened to John Henry or why the rowboat had been so completely destroyed. Mrs. Wiggins would not stay alone in the house and quickly moved back to Neu Boston. Edna May tried to sell the house but no one would buy it. The house stayed empty for several years and fell into disrepair. People gossiped that spirits speaking in a strange language haunted the old house. They thought because Mr. Wiggins had taken so many trips to China, maybe the strange language was Chinese! The gossip circulated through town and all the way to Neu Boston. The house became old and dilapidated. Windows were boarded up. The front screen door was broken and hanging off its hinges. Several of the shutters were missing while others creaked loudly as they swung in the slightest wind, banging against the side of the house. The roof leaked and the wooden siding badly needed a coat of paint. The mailbox post had rotted and fallen over and the front lawn became overgrown with weeds. Jackrabbits were now the only things living there and they seemed to multiply as fast as the weeds did. It was a very spooky place!

As time went on Louie built many of the buildings in town including a church and the town hall. All of his buildings were just a little bit crooked but since they were all crooked in the same way no one seemed to mind. The Town was called Marlowe after Silas Marlowe, its first selectman. The old Abnaki trails were widened several times and became streets. Eventually the horse drawn carriages gave way to trucks and cars. Part of the riverbank trail above the falls became Main Street, while the rest of the trail south to the bridge had a sign that read, "The Old Road To Marlowe." When Cyrus Phineas could no longer mill all of the grain the farmers brought to him, the farmers talked to the head of the Neu Boston and Maine Railroad. Tracks were laid between Main Street and the riverbank, all the way from Neu Boston to Mr. Phineas' gristmill. A narrow iron bridge was built across the Connecticut River just for the train right alongside the old covered wooden bridge. There was a small railroad station and loading platform built at the end of the track, next door to the old gristmill. Part of the station had a restaurant run by Ma Mitchell called the Whistlestop. It was a place where the locals got together for gossip and breakfast and gossip and lunch. The Whistlestop was the last building at the north end of town, except for Mr. Phineas' mill. It was also the last bus stop for the kids that went to the Marlowe Middle School.

Chapter Seven

A Hike with Mike

It was early one Saturday morning. The New England air was crisp, the sky clear and the rising sun meant it would soon be warmer. On the hillside above the river, bright maple and birch trees wore their full October colors pushing the dark pines into the background.

"What are the kids doing here? It's Saturday. There's no school," Net Bracey said to his friend Greeley Pierce.

"Don't know Net. They sure must know it's Saturday though, they're not walking as slow as they do during the week!"

Net Bracey and Greeley Pierce both worked for the Town Of Marlowe. They fished together off the Whistlestop Wharf often until the river freezes over in the winter.

"Seen Billy this morning?" Greeley asked Net.

"Nope... he's hidin' on us as usual. Just wait till he wants that fishin' shack out on the ice this winter. I've a good mind not to help!"

Net looked over at Billy's Bait Shack standing beside a half dozen old canoes.

"Think one of the canoes is missin' Greeley?"

"Can't tell."

Billy was short for Billy White Fox, the only Native American still living in Marlowe. He was the best fisherman on the river. During the summer season he put on a deerskin jacket and headband and reminded the townies to tell the rich folks from New York and Massachusetts that he was the only full-blooded Native American fishing guide on the river. And everyone at the Whistlestop had sworn not to tell about his degree from Dartmouth College. Billy also had an arrangement with Simpson's General Store to take most of their fishing supplies and sell the gear out of his fishing shack to his wealthy clients for higher prices than the town folks were willing to pay. Greeley and Net were always trying to find out where Billy caught the big fish, but somehow Billy always managed to keep it a secret.

Mike and Sam Marsh were the first to arrive at the wharf. They stopped and turned to watch the others walking quickly up Main Street. Nicole Amanto was carrying her cat Kramer in one arm, while holding her sister Ashley's hand with the other. Behind them were Jena and Kevin McMahon and their dog Loni. Kevin was still trying to start the zipper on his jacket while holding an old shovel under his arm. Suddenly, a black streak came out of the shadows behind the Whistlestop.

"Sam! I told you to put Christy in the house!" Mike yelled. "Now we've got two dogs and a cat!"

"I forgot," Sam said sheepishly as Christy licked hi hand and shuddered with the excitement of having her freedom.

Christy's attention turned quickly to Nicole's cat Kramer as she and Ashley arrived at the wharf, followed closely by Kevin's dog Loni. All the kids had on their school backpacks but today they carried no books, only lunch boxes and snacks.

Mike cupped his hands around his mouth and yelled, "Kevin, I told you not to bring Loni! You'll have to take her back home!"

Kevin was now trailing his sister Jena and still trying to start his zipper.

"Why! Christy's here!" Jena snapped back at Mike.

"This isn't going to work! You know how those dogs like to chase cats!"

"We're going for arrowheads, right Mike? Kevin said.

"Kevin! Didn't you hear me! Loni shouldn't be here!" Mike growled.

"Don't worry, I'll watch Loni," Kevin said as he stepped onto the wharf. "Besides, Loni won't go home if Christy 's here."

"I'll watch Christy," Sam offered.

"I'm not taking Kramer back home!" Nicole snapped. "You didn't let me take him on the last trip and both Christy and Loni went!"

Mike's head dropped to his chest as he wondered why he ever suggested going on a hike with these kids. Somehow he should have known that whatever he said to Sam and Kevin would simply go in one ear and out the other.

"Going for arrowheads, right Mike?" Kevin said again, oblivious to Mike's dejection.

"You two had better watch the dogs! Don't let them chase Kramer or we'll lose all of them!"

Sam and Kevin just looked at Mike, excited about going on a hike but not really paying attention to what he was saying.

"Let's go!" Jena said impatiently as she walked quickly away from the others and headed north up Main Street.

"Wait!" hollered Mike. "We're going south to the trail beside Chapin's Brook!"

Jena said nothing but turned on her heels and went south.

"Jena! Wait up! We have to stay together! You kids

better start listening to me or I'm going to call off this hike!" Mike stammered.

Jena began marching in place waiting for the others. The group moved south with the girls chattering and the boys more interested in who would be first behind Mike and Jena.

"What do we do when we get to the brook?" Kevin asked Mike.

"We'll follow it north to the foothills. The brook starts on Mount Sunapee."

"When are we going to eat?" Kevin asked

"Kevin, didn't you eat breakfast?"

"Yeah, but Mom packed these potato sticks in a can. They're like crispy French Fries. Really Good! Want to try some?"

"I thought you wanted to look for arrowheads, Kevin!"

"I do Mike but I get hungry thinking about those potato sticks."

"You're going to have to wait until we get to the base of the mountain. Think about arrowheads instead of potato sticks, Kevin."

Sam and Jena were ahead of Mike and the rest of the group when they reached the brook. The two of them started to climb over the metal guardrail when Mike yelled in an exasperated voice:

"Hold up! I don't want anybody falling in the brook! So stay on the trail and stay together!"

The gang had moved north for over an hour and then it happened! Kramer screeched and jumped out of Nicole's arms and headed off into the woods being chased by a barking Loni. Sam was able to grab Christy by the collar as Nicole and Kevin took off after the animals.

"NO! NO! Everybody stay together!" Mike stammered as he turned and sat down in the middle of the trail putting his head in his hands. "What's the use? I should have played basketball this morning!"

The voices of Nicole and Kevin yelling trailed off into the distance until they were no longer heard.

"What do we do now?" Ashley asked

"Just wait here," Mike replied. "I don't want anyone else getting lost! We'll wait here and hope they get back before too long."

"What if they don't come back?" Sam asked.

"Don't even think about it, Sam! We'll wait here as long as we can."

"Til it gets dark?" Jena asked, "I don't want to stay here in the dark!"

"No, we'll have to leave before dark to make sure we don't get lost. But aren't you worried about your brother, Jena?"

"He's my big brother and he's supposed to take care of me!"

Meanwhile Nicole had passed Kevin. Both were running through the woods as fast as they could to keep up with a barking Loni and Kramer ahead of them.

"Kramer, stop!!" Nicole yelled over and over.

Kevin was too short of breath to continue yelling. He heard splashing and saw Nicole jump over something ahead. As they ran off, Kevin came to a small stream. He stopped to catch his breath.

"I don't know if I can jump that far." Kevin said to himself.

He decided to take his shoes off and roll up his pant legs to cross the stream. By the time Kevin got to the other side and redressed himself, he could no longer see or hear Nicole and the animals. Kevin continued walking in the direction he had seen Nicole running, yelling her name.

"Kevin, where are you?" came back a faint cry.

"Keep yelling, Nicole! I can barely hear you!"

Kevin kept walking towards Nicole's voice until they could see each other.

"Come quick, Kevin! Kramer's disappeared!"

Kevin could now see Loni scratching the ground furiously with her front paws.

"Kramer went in there!" Nicole said pointing at where Loni was digging.

Kevin could see that the dog was trying to enlarge a hole in the steep ground ahead of him. Loni finally squeezed her way through the opening.

"Come out, Loni!" Kevin yelled into the hole.

Nicole then yelled for Kramer. Both took turns peering in the blackness and listening for the animals but heard nothing.

"Kevin, you have to make the hole bigger so I can go in."

"Sorry, Nicole, I dropped the shovel when we started chasing them."

"We'll have to use our hands."

"That will take a long time, Nicole."

"I don't care! I have to get Kramer!"

The two took turns digging with their hands to make the hole bigger until Nicole could wiggle herself inside.

"See anything?"

"It's too dark! Kramer, where are you?"

Nicole could hear a hissing sound echoing off the rock walls around her.

"Kevin, you have to come in here and help me. It's too dark!" Nicole said in a scared voice.

Kevin started digging again, stopping often to see how much of him he could get through the opening. He would try going in frontward and then backwards. Nicole was getting anxious.

"Come on, Kevin! It will be dark by the time you get in here. Then we won't be able to get back to the others!"

"I'm trying, Nicole!" said Kevin trying to back in butt first.

"Now you're blocking all the light, Kevin!"

"Whew! That was tough." He said finally getting the rest of his body through the hole.

"Feel around with your hands," Nicole's voice echoed.

"Jeez Nicole, this must be a big cave! Hey! Look ...arrowheads!"

A small shaft of light coming through the entrance allowed Kevin to spot three arrowheads on the dirt floor. As Kevin reached for one of them...it moved away from him and into the darkness. As he reached for the second and third they quickly moved out of sight also.

"Did you see that, Nicole? This place is haunted! There must be ghosts in here!"

Nicole was still feeling along the floor in the darkness. "Will you stop and help me find Kramer! I heard a hissing sound before. I know he's still in here."

A light brown tail suddenly flopped into the lighted floor area.

"Loni...it's Loni," Kevin sputtered grabbing her tail and pulling the dog to his side. "You're a bad girl! I told you not to chase Kramer!"

The dog looked sheepishly at Kevin knowing that she had caused trouble for him.

"Gotcha!" Nicole exclaimed as Kramer screeched and resisted by dragging her claws across the cave floor. "Let's get out of here!"

Kevin emerged last. Both could see that the afternoon shadows had grown long and it would soon be dark.

"I don't think we have time to find our way back to Mike before it gets dark. Think we should stay here? We may get lost, Nicole"

"We're lost now, Kevin! And I'm not going to stay in that cave all night!"

"We could stay here outside the cave. But then, there could be wolves out here tonight! Why don't we eat out here while it's still light and go back in and wait by the entrance until morning? I've got some potato sticks that my Mom packed," Kevin said excitedly as he opened the backpack he'd dropped beside the cave entrance. When they'd finished eating, Kevin went back into the cave.

As darkness approached Nicole reluctantly went back inside with Kevin. They were both tired from chasing the animals. Kevin fell asleep first.   hen

"Wake up, Kevin! Did you hear that?"

"What do you want, Nicole. I'm tired!"

"Voices, Kevin! There's somebody besides us in here!"

"I don't hear anything."

"Quiet and listen, Kevin!"

"Who are you?" came a low voice from the back of the cave.

"Oh my god! What is that, Nicole? Am I dreaming?"

"Who are you?" the voice shot back again in a more angry tone.

"Ah...we're Nicole and Kevin, sir."

"What are you doing in our cave?" came a voice that did not sound like the first one.

"Kramer came in here and we had to get hi   . And now it's getting dark. We have to stay here until morning."

"Who is Kramer?"

"My cat," Nicole answered. "Who are you?"

"Red Feather and Little Turtle. This is our cave! You must leave at first light!"

"Yes sir, we will," Kevin answered.

It took a long time for Nicole and Kevin to go to sleep.

Back on the trail to Sunapee, Mike and the rest of the group were getting anxious.

"We'd better start home soon. I don't want to be out here in the dark!" Jena declared.

"What about your brother?" Sam asked

"He'll be alright. Kevin's a Boy Scout."

"Where's Nicole?" Ashley asked

"She'll be alright, Kevin will take care of her. Besides they may be home already." Jena responded.

"Don't think so," Mike interrupted. "We're too far from home. I know they would have tried to find their way back here first. But it is getting late. We should start back and tell our parents what happened."

What was left of the gang started on their way home. Mike kept looking back in the direction they'd come hoping to see or hear something from the two missing kids. Mike didn't want to return home without Nicole, Kevin and the animals but felt there was no other choice.

Nicole was awakened by the stream of morning light falling across her face and the slapping of Loni's tail on the dirt floor of the cave. She sat up rubbing her eyes and looked around the cave.

"Kevin...wake up! Look at this!" Nicole said excitedly.

But Kevin kept on sleeping. She reached down and shook him as hard as she could.

"Wake up! There's a picture on the wall!"

"I'll look at in the morning." Kevin replied not even bothering to open his eyes.

"It is morning, Kevin! Open your eyes!"

Kevin rolled over on his back and looked at Nicole and then the cave wall.

"Jeez, Nicole...what is that?"

Nicole pointed at the cave wall, "It's a picture of a big snake!"

"Yeah! It looks like it's in the water. But what are those two ancient people doing? One looks like he's throwing a spear or something. This place is really weird Nicole. Arrowheads that move by themselves, voices, and now this strange picture! Do you see anyone in the back of the cave?"

Nicole squinted into the blackness at the back of the cave. "No, it's too dark. But we have to leave, Kevin. We told them we would."

"I'm hungry, Nicole. Do you have anything left to eat?"

"Kevin, you're always thinking about eating...and those dumb arrowheads!"

"Oh yeah, the arrowheads. Where did they go to?" Kevin looked around the cave floor but didn't see them. Then he spotted a small pile of old bones against the wall. He spread the debris with his hands. "There they are!" Kevin reached down and picked up the three arrowheads. They did not move this time. "These are good arrowheads for my collection. None of them are broken!"

"Quiet, Kevin! I hear some thing outside!"

Kevin put the arrowheads in his pocket and he and Nicole went outside. They could hear the faint sounds of someone yelling.

"That's my dad!" Nicole said excitedly picking up Kramer.

Kevin and Nicole started to walk towards the voice yelling as loud as they could, "Over here! Over here!" Loni took off ahead of them. They could see several people wearing bright clothes in the distance.

"I can see Mike and my dad and your dad, Kevin. I think its Jena and Uncle Scot and lots of other people. They sure got here early!"

"Nicole, I don't think we should tell anyone about the cave. Beside, if we tell them we slept in a haunted cave with the picture of a giant snake on the wall, they'd probably think we were crazy!"

"I won't tell."

When they reached each other, Nicole's dad Ron was the first to speak, "Are you alright, Nicole?"

"Yes. I just didn't sleep very good in that cave."

"Nicole! You weren't supposed to tell!!" Kevin whispered so loud everyone could hear.

"What cave, Kevin?" His dad Marc asked.

"Oh, it's nothing Dad...just a cave. Boy, I'm sure glad you found us. I was getting hungry."

The group started back to Marlowe.

"I found some more arrowheads, Dad." Kevin said proudly.

"That's great, Kevin. Where did you find them?"

"Oh... on the ground."

"You did not! You found them in the cave, Kevin!"

"Nicole!"

"Oh yeah, I forgot."

Nicole and Kevin walked the rest of the way home in silence, which was a hard thing for both of them to do.

Chapter Eight

The Game Of Benders

Days were getting shorter and the nights much colder. It was time for the kids to show up at the Whistlestop a little earlier each morning to wait for the school bus. The extra time was needed to go behind the Whistlestop to check the ice forming at the rivers edge. They would poke sticks through the ice to check its thickness. One morning Sam pulled out his stick and yelled, "It's time for Benders!"

"Oh...no. It's not ready. It's not thick enough!" stammered Phil Phineas

"Why do you care Phil? You never go out on the ice anyway!" Jena snapped back.

"Yeah the ice will never be thick enough for you. You're too fat!" Sam joked.

Jena put her stick at the edge of the ice and paced off six giant steps along the shore. "Who's got the other stick?" she said, still standing on one leg.

Mike reached down and placed his stick by her foot.

"I'm first!" Ashley said before the others could. She put one foot gingerly on the ice and then the other.

The ice creaked and cracked but didn't break! She slid one foot at a time slowly on the ice towards the second stick. The thin ice groaned and bent underfoot but she made it to the other stick without breaking through and getting her feet wet and everyone clapped. But they all knew that Ashley was the smallest and the lightest of them and that their test would be more difficult.

"Next!" Sam blurted out, as he slid a foot onto the ice. He had barely lifted his second foot onto the i e when the first foot went through. Sam jumped back and pulled out a wet shoe. "That's it for me!"

"Looks like it'll be awhile before anyone makes it across the cove." Mike said as the group turned and walked back towards the bus stop.

Only Phil Phineas remained behind, upset over what Jena and Sam had said. He thought for a moment and then addressed all the kids at the bus stop; "I'm going to offer a prize to the first person to make it all the way across the cove!"

"What's the prize?" Jena asked.

Phil hesitated, "Fifty Dollars!"

"Wow!" the group responded in unison.

"Do you need to be there?" Kevin asked.

"Of course!" Phil answered. Phil seemed proud of himself for the moment. He thought he'd really impressed the gang at the bus stop. But on the way to school with everyone still buzzing about the fifty-dollar prize, Phil's face grew longer. "Where am I going to get fifty dollars?" he thought to himself.

That day it seemed like everyone in the Marlowe Middle School was talking about the prize. Phil was being asked questions about it on his way to class, in class and after class. Phil tried hiding in the Boys Room and even in his locker, but he couldn't close the door. Waiting for the bus to go home that afternoon was another ordeal for Phil. He breathed a sigh of relief when Cookie's bus pulled up to the curb. Phil was the first one on and moved quickly to the back seat, not wanting to talk to anyone.

Once off the bus, Phil raced to his house and went directly to his room, and threw himself on the bed.

"Was that you, Phil?" his mother asked. "I have supper ready."

"I'm not hungry!"

"But Phil, you have to eat."

"Where am I going to get fifty dollars?" Phil asked himself again. His mother kept calling until Phil finally came down the stairs for supper. He was quiet the whole meal and never said anything to his parents about the prize.

When Phil arrived at the bus stop the next morning there were cars lined up on both sides of the street. It looked like the whole town of Marlowe was at the Whistlestop. Some of the oms were already taking their kids away soaking wet and giving the evil eye to Phil as he approached the gang at the rivers edge.

"How far did they get? Phil asked Mike.

"No one got very far. The ice is way too thin to make it across the cove."

Phil breathed a sigh of relief but knew he'd better have the fifty dollars before too long. "I'll have to ask my father tonight," he thought to himself, dejectedly. "I know he'll be mad, but there isn't anyone else."

That night at supper Phil almost asked the question of his father but ended up saying, "Would you please pass the salt, Dad?"

"Phil, what is wrong with you. Why do you keep asking me to pass the salt and pass the butter? And why are you being so polite?"

"Well Dad, I have a question," Phil said hesitantly.

"What is it for God's sake?"

"Can you give me fifty dollars?"

"Fifty dollars...for what?

"I'm giving this prize and I need the money."

"A prize for what? C'mon Phil...out with it!"

"For Benders."

"Why would you offer a fifty dollar prize? You know I hate that game. All it ever got you was wet feet. And someday someone is going to push his or her luck and fall through in the middle of the river! No you're never going to get prize money from me for that stupid game!"

Phil excused himself; "I can't eat anymore." He left the table and went to his room. "Now what do I do?"

The next morning Phil came down the stairs all dressed without his mother waking him, which was odd.

"You okay, Phil?" she asked.

"I'm fine, Mom. Would you drive me to school this morning? I'd like to get there early so I can study before class."

"Now, that's really odd!" Mrs. Phineas thought to herself, knowing how much Phil hated to study.

As they drove by the Whistlestop, Mrs. Phineas and Phil saw the crowds gathered behind the Whistlestop. She noticed Phil sliding further and further down in his seat as if he didn't want to be seen.

"Why are all those people there?" his mother asked.

"Don't know, Mom," Phil said sheepishly.

Phil waited outside on the front steps of the school as long as he could while everyone else went in, just so he wouldn't have to talk to anyone. The first bell had just rung when Ziggy Dimmit who was usually late, came bustling up the walkway and stopped beside Phil.

"What's a matter Phillsy? Why so glum? You're such a big man at school these days, giving that fifty dollar prize."

"Do you know where I can borrow some money, Zig?"

"Oh, I know. You don't have the prize money!"

"Shhhh! Somebody will hear you!"

"You can trust me to keep a secret, Phillsy." Ziggy thought for a moment, "I think I know where you can get the money."

"Where?" Phil asked, unsure that he should ask. Ziggy was an on again off again friend. Sometimes he acted like a friend and other times he made fun him.

"Down at the pool hall. I hear people borrowing money there all the time."

"Never been there," Phil responded.

"I'll take you there after school, if you want."

"Okay Zig. Meet you here after school." Phil replied as the two walked into the school together.

That afternoon Phil and Ziggy walked several streets south from the school and entered a building with a sign on front that read, 'Nelly's Pool Hall.' The smoke was thick inside and made Phil cough and his eyes start to water.

"It's okay Phillsy. My older brother, Denny, comes here all the time. There he is at that table over there! Hi Denny, this is my friend, Phillsy."

"What are you doing here Zig? You know ma will give me hell if she finds out you were here."

"We won't be long, Denny. We just came here so my friend could borrow some money."

The noise in the pool hall stopped suddenly and several cue sticks thumped on the floor when Ziggy said the word 'money.'

"How much money does your friend want to borrow?"

"Fifty dollars."

"That's a lot of money, Zig. What kind of collateral does your friend have?"

"What's that?"

"You know, something you can leave so that we know your friend won't run off with the money and not pay us back."

Denny's friend Snake Grasso leaned over and whispered in Denny's ear, "I know that Phil kid. His father owns the mill!"

"Kid, is your dad Cyrus Phineas?"

"Yes."

"Then why don't you borrow the money from him? He must be rich."

"He won't give it to me."

Snake whispered in Denny's ear again, "I've heard his father doesn't trust the bank.... probably keeps his money in the house. Find out what that key is for that's hanging from his belt."

"Well kid, we're going to need some kind of collateral if you want that much money. How about that key?"

"Oh no...I need it to open the front door in case my mom's not there when I get home from school."

Snake smiled at Phil, "That's okay kid, is your mom home today?"

"Yes she is."

"Well that'll work. Just leave the key here tonight while we round up the money. Don't want to spend time getting all that money together and then have you not come back now, do we? You'll get your key back tomorrow when you pick up the money."

Phil felt a little uneasy as he unbuckled his belt and handed Denny the key, but at least he would get his money.

After school the next day Phil and Ziggy returned to the pool hall. Denny saw them coming and met them at the door, "Here's your money and your key. It's two for one, you know."

"What's that mean?"

"It means you have thirty days to give us back two dollars for every one that we give you."

"I don't know...maybe you should take the money back. It may be longer than thirty days before anyone crosses the cove."

"Take the money kid. You have an honest face. We'll work something out."

As the kids left, Denny turned and winked at Snake who was turning a key over and over in his hand. A second key they had made at Jensen's Hardware Store!

"We need to talk where we won't be heard, Denny," Snake whispered.

They walked up the street from the pool hall to Memorial Park and sat on one of the benches. After making sure no one could overhear, Denny spoke "We've got to be careful breaking in. The police station is almost across the street from the mill! It'll have to be after midnight. Where do we hide out after we rob old man Phineas?"

"We'll wear masks, Denny. Nobody will know who we are. We won't need a hideout."

"But what if something goes wrong, Snake? Then we'll need a hideout."

"Okay...okay...what about that old house on Rabbit Run? Nobody's lived there for years."

"All right, Snake. If we're careful we probably won't need the hideout. When do we do it?"

"Tomorrow night."

"Why so soon?"

"The sooner the better!" sneered Snake Grasso.

The old church clock struck midnight as two figures moved quickly from one dark shadow to the next along Main Street, heading towards the old gristmill. Mr. And Mrs. Phineas were quite old and lived upstairs over the mill.

"Where's the key, Snake?"

"Shhh! Don't say my name, Denny! Somebody could be listening!"

"Okay Snake."

Snake had to pull up his ski mask to find the opening for the key. "Ahh...there it is!" Snake whispered as he turned the doorknob. The door started creaking as he opened it. They carefully climbed the stairs one at a time so they wouldn't be heard. Denny reached the top first and could see a light under the door. Snake pulled the ski mask over his face.

"On three," he whispered

On the count of three the two robbers burst into the room. Mr. and Mrs. Phineas were startled as they sat in their chairs watching television.

"Where's your money?" Snake snarled in a gruff voice pointing what looked like a gun in his pocket.

"I don't have any money here." Mr. Phineas replied in a shaky voice.

"Then where is your money?" Denny asked

"I don't keep it here, it's hidden."

"Take us to it now!" demanded Snake

"But I don't think we can find it in the dark." Mr. Phineas stammered.

Snake and Denny looked at each other, scratching their heads through their ski masks.

Finally Snake said, "Can you draw a map where it is?"

"Yes, I believe so."

Denny had Mrs. Phineas find a pencil and a piece of paper and told Mr. Phineas to draw the map. When he finished Snake grabbed the map, looked at it for a minute and then told Denny it was time to leave.

"Wait a minute, Snake. We can't leave these two here. The first thing they'll do is walk across the street to the police station!"

"Will you stop saying my name, Denny Dimwit! You might as well introduce us!"

"Sorry, Snake. And my name is Dimmit, not Dimwit, Snake!"

"Now we have to take them with us until we get the money."

"Okay you two, you're coming with us!" as Snake pulled Mrs. Phineas out of her chair and told them both to move ahead of them.

Downstairs, Snake told Denny to open the door and see if the coast was clear.

"Nobody there, Snake."

"Okay, out the door, you two!" Snake grunted as he pushed them through the front door.

No sooner were they out the door, than the headlights of a car turned onto Main Street and started heading towards them. Snake and Denny pulled the Phineas' back into the shadows holding their hands over their mouths. The slow moving car stopped every so often and the light from a flashlight would pan the doorway of each shop along Main Street.

"It's the sheriff, Snake! What do we do now?"

"Quiet! Get away from the doorway!"

But it was too late. The sheriff must have detected Denny moving and directed his flashlight to right where they were!

Sheriff McBean got out of the car and drew his revolver, "Alright, everybody step out of the shadows towards me, with your hands over your head!"

The two robbers released Mr. and Mrs. Phineas. Snake quickly reached into his pocket and threw the map back into the shadows. They all put their hands over their heads.

"Is that you, Mr. Phineas?" the sheriff asked.

"Yes Windy, it's me. These two were trying to rob us!"

Sheriff McBean handcuffed Snake and Denny and took them to the station. After they were booked, the sheriff asked both of them, "Mr. Phineas says you forced him to draw a map. Where is it?"

Snake and Denny looked at each other.

"We don't have a map, sheriff. Don't know what Mr. Phineas is talking about."

Sheriff McBean knew they were lying and decided to lock up the prisoners and have his deputies look for the map in the morning.

Several deputies scoured the area where the sheriff had caught Snake and Denny but the map wasn't found.

"There was a lot of wind that night. No telling where that map went to," offered one deputy.

About a week later, Snake and his buddy Denny were transferred to the state prison in Neu Boston to await trial.

Mr. Phineas was very angry with Phil when he learned Phil had given their key to strangers. But Phil didn't mind the lecture. He had his fifty-dollar prize money and with Denny and Snake in jail he knew he wouldn't have to pay it back!

"I'm sorry Dad, I won't let it happen again," Phil said trying to hide a smile.

The next morning Phil couldn't get to the Whistlestop fast enough. The crowd of people trying to get the prize was now smaller. Several kids were already out on the ice but not very far from shore. Jena had walked away from the crowd and into the bushes looking for good bender sticks to mark the start and the finish line for the game that day. Something had been caught in the bush she was standing in front of. It was a white piece of paper, difficult to see with all the snow on the ground. She picked it out of the bush, brushed it off and looked at it quickly before stuffing it in her pocket.

"It looks like a pirates treasure map!" She said to herself, looking around to make sure no one had watched her pick it up.

Suddenly Ashley came streaking across the beach and out on the ice, surprising everyone! She got about halfway across the cove when she screamed. Everyone heard the ice break and watched Ashley fall into the water.

"Quick Sam, run to the Whistlestop and tell Ma Mitchell to call the fire department!"

Sam disappeared into the restaurant and a short time later the fire truck sirens could be heard coming from Main Street. The firemen worked quickly, pulling several lengths of ladder off the side of the truck and laying them end to end on the ice. One of the firemen got down on his knees and began crawling his way to Ashley on top of the ladders.

"I'm coming Ashley, just hang on!" the fireman shouted. But Ashley kept on screaming and flailing her arms trying to stay afloat! Then for some unknown reason Ashley stopped screaming. Her head was above water and she seemed very calm.

"I've got you," the fireman said as he grabbed one of Ashley's arms. She was too heavy to pull up on top of the ladder. The fireman began using his axe with one hand to break the ice while he held Ashley with the other hand. Gradually they worked their way towards shore until the ice was thick enough to support another fireman who quickly helped pull Ashley out of the water. Everyone clapped as one of the other firemen covered Ashley with a blanket and took her into the Whistlestop. Ma Mitchell helped her out of the wet clothes, wrapped her in a dry blanket and sat her in front of the fire. Outside the fireman who'd gone out on the ladder was sitting on a rock and taking off his big black boots because his feet had gotten wet. He pulled the first one off, turned it upside down and watched the water run out of it. He did the same with the second boot but with the water that ran out came a small leaf, a small green leaf that floated back into the river with the water from the boot.

Chapter Nine

The Jailbreak

With the game of Benders shut down for the rest of this year, there was no more excitement on the river behind the Whistlestop. There was nothing for the kids to do except shiver outside the restaurant waiting for the school bus.

"The kids will freeze out there!" Ma Mitchell said trying to scrape an opening in the frosted over front window. "Kids...c'mon in here where it's warm! Cookie will blow his horn when he gets here."

The words were hardly out of her mouth when the kids came storming through the door followed by the noise of their backpacks hitting the floor and table-tops. Greeley Pierce, Net Bracey and Reverend Anderson were sitting at the counter swapping the latest Internet jokes. Their voices quieted down as the kids stampeded into the Whislestop. The sound of a motor was heard shutting off outside.

Ma looked out the window again, "It's just the sheriff."

Sheriff McBean had the Neu Boston News tucked under his arm as he took up the stool next to Greeley.

"The usual, Ma."

Ma Mitchell nodded as Windy unfolded his newspaper on the counter. As she tried to find a spot on the counter for his coffee cup the sheriff suddenly jumped up off his stool, surprising Ma who was now pouring coffee all over the newspaper instead of in his cup!

"My God...how did those two dummies escape from prison? Denny and Snake together don't have enough brains to come in out of the rain! I've got to find them. They'll probably come back here for Mr. Phineas' money! Greeley, Net...I'm deputizing both of you to help me find them!"

"But sheriff, we're not cops!" Greeley pleaded. Besides, we've got work to do down at the town garage."

"All I ever see you doing in the garage is play cards. This is more important. We'll search the south end of town first. That's the direction they'll be coming from."

Greeley and Net went reluctantly with the sheriff as Cookie pulled up in the big yellow school bus and took the kids to school.

The sheriff and his two deputies showed up at the Whistlestop early each morning, but they had no luck finding the two escaped convicts. After three days no one in the restaurant even bothered to ask if they'd been found. They could tell the question really irritated the sheriff.

One morning Billy White Fox came through the door and walked up to Greeley and Net. "Where have you two been? The ice on the river is plenty thick. It's time to get the shack out on the river."

Greeley and Net looked at the sheriff.

"Okay, it's been five days and we're not getting anywhere looking for Snake and Denny, might as well help Billy."

"We'll help, but you have to take us to your secret fishin' hole. You promised last year, but you didn't do it."

"I did! You just don't know how to fish."

"No more funny stuff, Billy. This time you have to show us where it is or we're not helping!"

"But that fishin' hole is my livelihood!"

"Then it's your choice, Billy. Show us where it is next spring or give up ice fishin' this year!"

Billy knew he was in a bind. The town truck was the only vehicle powerful enough to pull his shack out on the ice. "Okay, you guys win!"

"You heard sheriff. He's got to show us in the spring!"

McBean nodded that he'd heard the promise.

"I'll get the truck, Billy," Net said. "You and Greeley get the shack ready."

Billy went into the shack and brought out a roll of rope that was so heavy he could hardly carry it. They uncoiled one end and tied it across the wooden runners that supported the shack floor. Then Greeley started to uncoil the rest of it.

"What are you doing?" Billy snapped.

"Lookin' for weak spots."

"It's the same darn rope we used last year and it worked fine."

"Okay Billy, don't get huffy!"

Net pulled the truck alongside the shack and Billy tied the other end of the rope to the bumper. Greeley climbed into the passenger side of the truck and Billy motioned them to move the truck onto the ice. When all the slack was out of the rope the shack started to move onto the ice.

"Where are you going?" Billy hollered at them. "You're too far up-river! They do this to me every year!" Billy thought to himself.

The truck stopped and Net stuck his head out the window, "Can't go too close to the falls. Ice is too thin!"

"Then we're going to have to push it closer by hand!"

Net turned the steering wheel to get the shack closer to the falls. When the shack was in the middle of the river, Billy untied the rope and Greeley helped him wind it and hang it on a peg on the outside of the shack.

Net and Greeley yelled back at Billy as they drove off, "Don't forget your promise, Billy!"

The kids waiting to be picked up and the rest of the people inside, watched the moving of the shack from the Whistlestop rear window. They continued to look out the window as Billy got busy making a series of holes through the ice with his hand auger and putting out his tip-ups. He had just put in his third tip-up when the flag went up on the first. Billy pulled up his first fish of the winter season. He held the fish over his head and slapped it loudly against his open hand.

"What's he doing?" Nicole asked

"Keep watching." Ma answered

It wasn't long before a large bird, an eagle, came swooping in and took the fish out of Billy's hand.

"Jeez...did you see that? It was an eagle!" Sam said excitedly.

Cookie pulled the big yellow bus in front of the Whistlestop and blew the horn. Slowly the kids came straggling out and boarded the bus. That afternoon on the way back from school Kevin whispered to Mike sitting beside him, "Mike would you talk to Mr. White Fox for us?"

"About what? And who is us?"

"Me and Nicole...it's about a secret. Can't tell you until you promise."

Jena's ears perked up, "What secret?"

"It's nothin' Jena. If I tell then it won't be a secret."

"I can't talk to him unless I know what you want to talk about!" Mike snapped back.

Kevin cupped his hand over Mike's ear and whispered, "It's about a haunted cave that has a drawing of a giant snake and two ancient people on the wall.

Nicole and me found it! We'll take you and Mr. White Fox there. The ancient people could be Mr. White Fox's ancestors. He might know what the picture means."

"Is this another one of your lame jokes, Kevin?"

"No Mike. There really is this cave. It's where Nicole and me stayed the time we got lost chasing the animals on the hike. You remember!"

"How could I forget?" Mike replied. "Okay, I'll ask him, but I have to go too!"

The next morning when Ma motioned the kids to come inside Kevin told Mike, "Stay here Mike, we need to talk to Mr. White Fox."

Jena noticed that her brother and Nicole stayed outside with Mike. "What are you guys up to?"

"Nothing, Jena… it's a secret I can't tell you about right now. Why don't you go inside with the others?" Kevin responded.

"I have a secret, too!" Jena said, not wanting to leave. "You tell me your secret and I'll tell you mine!"

"You're making it up, Jena!"

"No I'm not. I found a pirate map!" Jena blurted out and then covered her mouth with her hand when she realized she'd given away her secret.

"Okay, let's go." Mike said as Jena walked into the Whistlestop in a huff.

Billy looked up as the three approached the ice shack.

"You here for Ma's fish?" Billy asked as he baited one of his tip-ups.

"No," Mike answered. "We want to show you something. These two say they found a secret cave with a picture on the wall…a picture of a giant snake!"

"Interesting," Billy responded as he pulled up a fish from one of the tip-ups. "Where's the cave?"

"We'll take you there," Nicole answered.

Billy removed the hook and held out the fish. "Anyone want to feed Swift Wing?"

Nicole reached for the fish. Billy helped her hold the fish over her head and slap it against an open hand. Billy pointed north up the river and the kids watched a speck coming towards them out of a patch of distant trees. When it got closer you could see it had a white head and dark wings, the eagle swooped down and snatched the fish from Nicole's hands and started back to her nest!

"Wow!" Kevin said excitedly, "Can I feed the Eagle?"

"Sorry, You'll have to come back tomorrow. No more feeding him today," Billy said. "Now let's go see this cave."

"We've got to go back on the trail where Loni and Kramer ran away." Kevin offered.

Mike remembered just where it was. When they reached the spot, Kevin began trying to retrace the path he and Nicole and the animals had taken. Kevin kept looking up at the trees ahead of him.

"What are you looking for?" Mike asked.

"A blue sock...when I took my shoes off to cross the brook one of my socks fell in the brook and I hung it on the branch of a tree to dry and forgot it on the way home. It's close to the cave."

"There it is!" Nicole said pointing to one of the trees ahead.

Meanwhile, not far from Billy and the three kids a voice whispered, "Snake did you hear that?"

"Yeah, I can see three kids and Billy White Fox," said Denny looking through the trees. "They're coming this way. We'd better hide in the woods until they leave."

"That's it!" Kevin said excitedly. Shortly afterward they found the opening to the cave in the foothills of the mountain just ahead.

Nicole was the first to enter the cave.

Inside Kevin pointed at the picture on the wall, "What do you think of that?" He said to Billy and Mike.

"That's awesome! That snake is so big!" Mike responded. "Looks like it was made a long time ago." Mike said as they all watched Billy studying the drawing in detail

"It's not a snake," Billy said after a long pause. "It's an eel. I'm an Abnaki. My mother told me about two young braves who were killed by the Mohawks' giant eel a long time ago. The Mohawks were our enemy then and their shaman, Black Dog, commanded the beast. The eel attacked a group of Abnakis in canoes and bit the right arm of the Abnaki chief called Graywolf who never regained the use of his arm and would never again lead his braves into battle. This picture was probably done by some Abnaki brave who was frustrated because the tribe was never able to take revenge against the Mohawks."

"You know a lot about your ancestors, Billy. What ever happened to them and the giant eel?" Mike asked.

"Don't know what happened to the eel. The Mohawk camp was far downstream, where the Ashweelot meets the Connecticut. Our village used to be right above the falls on the river where our town is now. But they left here years ago. There was a mysterious death of two young braves. One of them was the son of Chief Graywolf, the one injured by the eel. He was called Little Turtle, and was to become our tribe's shaman. We know from the Pequot's that Black Dog was afraid Little Turtle would become too powerful but could never connect him with the boys deaths. It is a long story but the spirits of the dead boys haunted our village so much that they moved the campsite further north on the river."

"What was the other boys name?" Kevin asked.

"Don't remember now...but I will," Billy responded looking down at a pile of half burned wood on the cave floor. "Did you guys start a fire?"

"No," answered Nicole. "We didn't have any matches."

"Strange," Mike thought. "Wonder who else has been using this cave?"

There were lots of questions for Billy as they started back. When the group reached the trail Billy stopped. "You guys continue home. I want to look around a bit."

The kids were surprised that Billy did not want to return to town with them.

"Can we come and feed the eagle tomorrow?" Nicole asked.

"Yes. You can all feed Swift Wing. I'm at the shack every morning. Just don't want any of you to miss the bus or I'm in trouble with Cookie!"

Billy watched until the three kids were out of sight. He was concerned about the pile of burnt wood in the cave. Someone had been there recently and he didn't want the kids with him as he searched the woods around the cave. On his way back to the cave, Billy stopped by the stream where Kevin had left his sock. There were two different footprints in the snow near the brook.

"One of them could have been Mike's," He thought. "The second is too big for the other kids, so there were at least one and possibly two adults here recently."

Billy continued to examine the area around the cave, finding several freshly broken branches and more footprints in the snow, probably from when they were gathering firewood. Billy finally thought there was no more to be learned and started home.

Meanwhile the kids talked about the picture and what Billy had said to them as they walked the trail back to Marlowe. No one noticed the shadowy figures following, hiding behind trees as the kids walked the trail home.

"I've got some snacks left in my backpack," Kevin offered. "Why don't we stop here for a rest?"

Without saying anything, Nicole sat down on the nearest log. Kevin sat beside her and Mike looked for another spot to sit.

"How are you going to keep this a secret from your sister?" Mike asked.

"I don't know. She'll probably tell my mom if I don't tell her, but then she'll blab it to everyone if I do tell her."

"Wait...didn't she say she had a secret?" Nicole asked.

"Yeah, she said she found a pirates map. But maybe she just made it up."

"Why don't you ask her to show you the map? Then you'll know." Mike offered.

"If she has a map then tell her we'll blab her secret if she blabs about ours!"

"Okay, when my mom picks her up after school tomorrow and I get home from soccer practice." Kevin answered.

Meanwhile, Snake who heard every word, whispered to Denny, "His sister has the map!"

Snake and Denny retreated as the kids picked up their backpacks and headed back to Marlowe.

"We can't go back to the cave, those kids will be back." Snake said angrily. "We need a new hideout and need to get the map from that kid's sister."

"I know just the place!" Denny exclaimed. "We'll use that old dilapidated house on Rabbit Run Road! Nobody would ever look for us there! Maybe we can get my truck back, too. I left it behind the pool hall. There's a key under the bumper and we can use the truck to kidnap the kid!"

Chapter Ten

Spirits From the Past

D enny and Snake crept into town that night. It was a
perfect night for crooks. An icy rain was coming
down hard and no one was out on the streets. The cold,
wet winter had formed large icicles that hung from every
roof and the freezing rain only made them longer.

The two crooks entered the old Wiggins house
through a broken rear cellar window. They felt their
way upstairs in the darkness, trying every light switch
along the way.

"No electricity, Snake. No heat either. It's colder
than the cave in here!"

It seemed to take a long time but Snake finally
found old candles and matches in one of the bureau
drawers. They went through the closets and found a
lot of men and women's clothes.

"I have a plan," Said Snake. "Remember that Kevin
kid said their mother picked Jena up after school. I'm
going to dress up like a woman and meet Jena at the
bus stop."

"What about her mother?"

"That's where you come in, Denny. Pick out some of the
men's clothes that fit you. Then we'll go get your truck."

On the way to school the next morning, Denny's black truck was parked on Main Street watching the kids leave their houses and make their way to the bus stop. No one paid any attention to the man and woman sitting in the truck.

"Denny, there's the kid and his sister. We need to find out were they live." said Snake quickly jumping out of the cab.

Snake had on a big floppy hat, a long yellow dress and high heels as he walked unsteadily up to Kevin and Jena and spoke in a high-pitched voice, "Hey kids...do you know of any houses for sale in Marlowe? My husband and I are new in town."

"No, we don't know any." Kevin answered a little startled to be approached by a stranger this early in the morning.

"Well, you two look as though you must live in a nice neighborhood. Where do you live? Maybe we can look there?"

"We live in the brick house on Beaver Pond Road," Jena offered quickly.

"Thank you dear," the woman answered, patting Jena on the head and walking back across the street towards the truck.

"Jena, you know what mom said. We shouldn't talk to strangers!"

"Well, you talked to her!" Jena said scowling at her brother who said nothing.

Snake and Denny watched as the kids all gathered in front of the Whistlestop and then drove off.

That afternoon, Denny parked his truck up the street from Kevin and Jena's house.

"That must be their car in the driveway. Don't see anyone around. You know what to do, Denny!"

Denny walked slowly up to the house then quickly moved to the front of the car, raised the hood, stuffed something in his coat pocket and came back to the truck. He pulled a handful of spark plug wires out of his pocket and showed them to Snake.

"Yeah, that ought to do it, Denny."

Denny then drove off and parked the truck so they could watch the bus stop.

After a time Cookie pulled the big bus in front of the Whistlestop. The kids got off a lot quicker than they'd gotten on that morning. Some were walking down Main Street in small groups, while others were being picked up in cars. Cookie the bus driver noticed the woman approach Jena who was now standing alone on the sidewalk.

"Your mother is having car trouble, child. She asked me to walk you back to your house," Snake explained.

Jena reluctantly took the woman's hand and they started following the others down Main Street.

Cookie watched all the kids leave the bus. He saw the woman offering Jena her hand and knew it wasn't her mother. "Must be okay," Cookie thought to himself. "Jena seems to know her, but I've never seen her before."

When Cookie turned the bus around and headed north on Main Street, Denny started the truck and pulled up behind Snake and Jena. Snake put his hand over Jena's mouth and grabbed her as Denny opened the truck door. They waited until the kids left Main Street and then went back to the old Wiggins house. They took Jena to a room in the middle of the house with no windows. Snake motioned her to sit down as he took off his hat and wig. Jena looked startled to see that Snake was a man. "Okay kid, where's the map?"

"What map? I don't have any map!"

"Don't lie, kid. We know you've got the map!"

"I want to call my mom," Jena said.

"You can talk to your mom after we get the map." Snake snapped. "Where is it?"

"It's at my house. Let me go and I'll bring it to you,"

"Not so fast kid, we're going with you but we'll have to wait until dark. Don't want to run into McBean again!"

Meanwhile Mrs. McMahon ran across the street when she saw the neighbor children coming.

"Where's Jena?" she asked.

"Don't know," The kids answered. "She was waiting for you at the bus stop."

"My car wouldn't start. I'm going to call Sheriff McBean. Jena should have come home by now!"

The sheriff arrived at the McMahon house and talked to Mrs. McMahon.

"The neighbor kids said that Jena got off the bus with them but she hasn't come home and I need to find her!"

The sheriff and Mrs. McMahon drove back to the bus stop slowly but there was no sign of her. McBean knew where the school bus driver lived and drove to his house. Cookie told them about the woman he'd never seen before, but thought that Jena knew her after taking her hand.

"I don't like the looks of this," the sheriff said. "Let's go back to your house and find out why your car didn't start."

"I want to go with you." Cookie insisted, feeling guilty that he hadn't stopped the woman with Jena to find out who she was.

McBean opened the hood and saw the missing spark plug wires, "This is serious!" he told Mrs. McMahon.

The sheriff and Cookie drove off to round up a bigger search party for Jena. He and the bus driver spent the rest of the afternoon with his deputies, scouring the town for any signs of Jena, and stopping and asking people if they had seen her and this unknown woman. By late afternoon, the sheriff had organized a search party and had people tacking up pictures of Jena all over town. The whole town was buzzing about Jena McMahon's disappearance.

Billy stopped in the Whistlestop after checking his tip-ups for fish. He saw Jena's picture taped to the door of the restaurant. "What's this, Ma... one of your kids missing?"

"Yes Billy, she never came home from school today. Cookie said he dropped her off here but that was the last time she was seen."

"You know Ma, I was just with three of those kids, but she wasn't one of them." Then Billy thought about the footprints near the cave. "It may be nothing but I should tell McBean about it."

Billy walked behind Ma's counter and picked up the telephone. "Sheriff, I heard about the missing girl and thought I should call."

"What is it Billy?"

"It might not mean anything, but three of the kids took me to a cave north of town. There were fresh footprints near the cave...one, maybe two people. Whoever it was may have been using the cave. Someone tried to start a fire and the kids said it wasn't them."

"Why did you say one or two, Billy?"

"They were large prints and they were different, Sheriff. One of them could have been from Mike

Marsh. He's a big kid. No! Come to think of it, Mike was wearing boots and both of these were shoe prints. There were two of them."

"I was afraid of that, Billy!"

"Why?"

"I didn't say anything to the McMahon's but there was a jailbreak in Neu Boston this week. It was those two hoodlums that tried to rob old man Phineas. Don't know why the McMahon girl would be involved, but they could have come back here. Would you help us search the area? You know those woods better than anyone, Billy."

"Of course, sheriff...when and where should I meet you?"

"Meet us at the McMahon house at eight in the morning."

"I'll be there."

When the sheriff arrived at the McMahon house there were two reporters and a camera crew waiting. Mr. and Mrs. McMahon and the sheriff went on the evening news asking for people's help in finding Jena. The sheriff said the search party would be forming at the McMahon house at eight o'clock and that people helping should wear clothes suitable for hiking. Everyone in Marlowe and Neu Boston knew about Jena. Unfortunately Snake and Denny also saw the news that night! Denny had a small battery powered television he used on camping trips and had set it up in the Wiggins house.

"Clothes for hiking!" Snake said clapping his hands together. "They're searching the woods tomorrow! We can go to the kid's house as soon as they all leave in the morning! Denny, I want you to park the truck so you can see when they leave, but make sure nobody sees you! Then you come back here and we'll take the kid and go get the map!"

"Okay, Snake," Denny replied.

When the sheriff arrived at the McMahon house the next morning, there was a crowd of people, some inside, some outside. Jena's brother and all her cousins were inside along with Billy, Net, Greeley, Cookie and several others. The cousins were all looking at family pictures Mrs. McMahon had put on the bulletin board in the kitchen.

"There's a picture of the rabbit house!" Sam said excitedly. "That's where we had the Easter egg hunt!"

"Yeah, no one mows the grass there so it's a perfect place to hide Easter eggs. Besides, having all the rabbits around makes it seem more like Easter." Mrs. McMahon explained. "But that's enough small talk, We need to go look for Jena."

"Quiet!" Mr. McMahon hollered above the noise of the crowd. "Let the sheriff talk!"

"Your attention, everyone! I need your attention!" the sheriff shouted. "We're going to search the woods north of town, off the trail to Sunapee. Billy White Fox and me will give you more instructions when we get there. You can follow him. We'll have to leave our cars in the field next to the trail where it goes across Main Street. Cookie, I want you to take the kids to school as usual. I don't want them on the search. The last thing I want to happen is to lose another kid in the woods!"

"But sheriff, I want to go on the search myself!" Cookie said.

"And I want to help look for my sister!" Kevin exclaimed.

"We want to help find Jena Too. She's our cousin!" the rest of the kids shouted.

"No! No!" McBean yelled back. "I will not take the chance of losing another child! Now take them to school, Cookie!"

Cookie led an angry bunch of kids out the front door to the school bus while the rest of the group got in cars and headed south on Main Street. No one noticed the black truck on the next street. It pulled away from the curb almost as soon as the school bus and the search party cars left.

Billy led the group up the trail to the cave site. He and the sheriff organized teams of people to search areas around the cave and report back. The search took only about an hour, but no new clues were found. No new signs of who had been there or that they had anything to do with Jena!

She's not here," Billy said dejectedly. "Let's not waste any more time."

"I want to start searching the outskirts of town. There are a number of old, abandoned farm buildings there." The sheriff added. "Let's go back and meet at the Lakeview Farm. We'll spread out from there."

"Good," Billy said. "I can check my tip-ups on the way back. It won't take me long. I'll catch up with you there."

Meanwhile, back on the school bus, "I'm not going to school! I'm going to look for my sister Jena!" Kevin said angrily.

"Me to!" the others said one by one.

"Now kids, I can't go against the sheriff's orders! I'd like to go on the search also, but I have to take you to school." said Cookie shoving the kids one by one onto the bus.

He closed the door and turned the bus around and headed towards the middle school, but the yelling didn't stop.

"Why are you afraid of the sheriff, Cookie?" Mike asked.

"Yeah, he's just a pussycat," Sam added.

"What can he do to you? Put you in jail?" Nicole asked.

"Yeah, if he puts you in jail then there'd be nobody to drive the school bus. He couldn't do that!" Kevin explained.

"If you really wanted to help, you'd turn this bus around and go where they're looking for Jena!" Ashley added.

"But I do want to help kids! Really! I feel awful that I didn't find out who the woman was that took Jena's hand. I should have!" Cookie said still angry at himself.

"Well you don't feel bad enough to look for Jena. You only feel bad enough to take us to school!" Mike countered.

"Alright, that's enough!" said Cookie as he turned the bus around and headed south.

The boys were high fiving each other and hollering while the girls clapped.

"If I end up in McBean's jail for this, you'd better all come visit me." Cookie smiled. "I left my hiking boots at your house, Kevin. I was going to change my shoes at your house for the search. I just forgot them when McBean changed plans on us. It'll just take a minute to stop and put them on.

Cookie stopped the bus in front of the McMahon house and turned to the kids. "You can stay on the bus or come in. I'm just going to change my shoes."

They all followed Cookie up the front walk and into the house. Cookie sat down and began changing to his hiking boots.

"Sam, did you take the picture of the rabbit house? It's gone!" Kevin complained.

"I did not! I didn't touch it!" Sam replied angrily as he walked closer to the bulletin board. "It's right there, Kevin. It just fell onto your arrowhead collection."

Kevin looked down at the picture. "Hey,...look at this!"

"What is it?" Cookie asked as he finished lacing his hiking boots.

"Three arrowheads aren't pointing the way they should. They're all pointing right at the picture of the rabbit house!" Kevin answered.

Cookie and all the kids gathered around to see what Kevin was so excited about.

"The picture must have hit the arrowheads when it fell, that's all Kevin."

"I don't think so," Kevin responded, remembering the strange movement of the three arrowheads in the cave. He just wasn't sure if those were the same arrowheads.

Cookie noticed the wide-eyed expression on Kevin's face. "If you think it means something, Kevin we'll check it out. I'm already in hot water anyway."

The noise of a car engine was heard pulling into the McMahon's driveway. It was Billy on his way to check his tip-ups. He'd seen the school bus parked outside the McMahon house and knew it shouldn't be there.

"Cookie, why didn't you take the kids to school?" Billy asked.

"Don't ask, Billy. It's a long story," returned Cookie.

"I thought something had surfaced when I saw the bus here."

"No. We were just heading out to find you." Cookie told Billy.

"The search party has already left the woods. She's not there. We're going to search the old abandoned farms on the outskirts of town. Everyone is meeting at Lakeview Farm. I'm just going to check the tip-ups and then I'm going straight there." Billy offered.

"Can we go with you?" Sam asked. "And watch you feed the eagle?"

"I'm not a school bus, Sam. I can only fit three or four of you in my car," Billy answered. "It would go faster if some of you would help check the tip-ups, though."

"That'll work, Billy. Kevin and I need to check something out before we head for the farm. You take the rest of them and we'll meet you there." Cookie offered.

Billy drove off in his car with Mike, Nicole, Sam and Ashley, while Cookie and Kevin took the school bus towards Rabbit Run Road. When Cookie turned into the north end of the road he stopped the bus.

"There's a black truck in front of the old Wiggins place, the rabbit house as you guys call it, but nobody lives there! I've seen that truck before. Where was it?" Cookie was talking out loud. "I remember. It was parked on Main Street. It was there yesterday when Jena got off the bus! We've got to be careful, Kevin. I'm not taking the bus any closer."

"Then let's walk there," Kevin said

"Maybe we should go get the sheriff instead," Cookie replied.

"We don't even know if Jena is in there, Cookie," Kevin countered as he pulled the handle to open the bus door.

"Wait!" Cookie whispered as he followed Kevin who was now almost to the front porch.

The old porch stairs creaked loudly as Kevin stepped onto them. He was careful not to step into any holes in the porch floorboards, many of which were rotted or broken. Cookie hid by the side of the house as Kevin approached one of the boarded up windows and tried to see inside through a crack between the boards.

"Can't see anything, Cookie...it's too dark in there."

Kevin walked to the broken screen door covering the big door behind it. The bottom screen was torn so Kevin could reach his hand through and turn the doorknob. It opened!

"Kevin, don't go in there!" Cookie whispered as loud as he could, watching him disappear inside.

There was a lot of noise inside now and Cookie didn't know what to do. He waited but Kevin didn't come out.

"I'm not going in there. I've got to go get the sheriff."

As Cookie headed back to the bus he heard the squeaking noise of the old screen door opening and then slam shut. He jumped behind the nearest tree and watched as he saw Jena and Kevin being pushed ahead of two men towards the black truck. He watched the kids go into the truck and sit between the two men. As the truck pulled away from the house, Cookie ran back to the bus. The black truck was moving fast down the street away from him.

"What do I do now?" Cookie said over and over to himself. "It's too late to get the sheriff!"

Meanwhile Billy and the rest of the gang had arrived at the ice shack. Billy and each of the kids began hauling up the lines and checking them for fish. They heard barking in the distance and Sam could see Kevin and Jena's dog, Loni, heading towards the ice shack.

"Somebody let out Kevin's dog again," Mike said. "Maybe we should take her with us to help search the old farms. She might be able to find Jena better than we could."

"Okay Mike...let her stay. We don't have time to take her back home anyway." Billy quipped.

Ashley pulled up the first fish but wanted Billy to take it off the hook. He then had Ashley hold the fish over her head and slap it against an open palm. Everyone watched as Swift Wing came quickly and took her meal.

Mike pulled up another fish on the next to last tip-up, "Got one, Billy. What should I do with it?"

"Hang it on one of the pegs on the side of the shack."

Mike saw that the fish had swallowed the hook so he cut the line. He wrapped the fishing line several times around the peg and left it hanging there. He was about to leave the shack with Billy and the others when they heard the ice cracking and looked to see a strange green glow under the ice holes. Whatever it was seemed to be moving round and round the shack faster and faster under the ice! They just stood there as the cracks spread from one hole to the next!

Cookie started the bus as he watched the black truck turn left heading towards Main Street. He backed up and turned the steering wheel until the bus also pointed towards Main Street. He saw the truck bear left again onto Main heading north back towards him. He floored the engine of the big yellow bus to get to Main Street as fast as he could. Cookie quickly turned south on Main Street. He could see the truck in the distance coming directly towards him!

"They've got both kids. I can't let them get away!"

As the two vehicles approached each other, Cookie could see the faces of the two men and the kids sandwiched between them. They were about to pass each other right in front of the Whistlestop, when Cookie blew the bus horn as loud as he could and swerved the bus into the side of Denny's truck! The bus stopped, but the truck was pushed off the road with it's hood popped open and headed down the riverbank past the Whistlestop towards the ice. Sparks were flying everywhere as the truck careened off rocks and boulders on its way to the river. It slammed into a large boulder and both doors flew open. Snake, who was sitting in the passenger seat was thrown out onto the ice and lay there unconscious. Denny was slumped over the steering wheel.

"Quick, Kevin! Get out!" Jena said pushing him out the open passenger door. "Run to the ice shack. I can see Mike and the others!"

Denny moaned as he raised his head and opened his eyes. He saw the kids running away, and then Snake lying outside on the ice. "Wake up, Snake. They're getting away!"

Snake pulled himself up on the open door and into the cab. Denny's tires were smoking and squealing as it slid and swerved, chasing Jena and Kevin across the ice.

Chapter Eleven

The Rivers Dark Secret

B illy and the kids at the shack heard the crash between Cookie's bus and the truck. They watched as the truck slammed into the boulder. They could see someone lying outside on the snow and both doors on the truck open. Jena and Kevin came out of the truck and started running at them. Then the truck started up and began chasing Jena and Kevin, slipping and sliding on the ice with tires smoking!.

"Quick Jena!" Sam hollered at her.

The rest of the kids at the shack began yelling too, barely hearing themselves above the roar of the truck. Billy looked down and noticed the green glow was trying to push through the ice under his feet. Now there were cracks in the ice between all of Billy's fishing holes. Everyone felt the ice under their feet raise up, but couldn't take their eyes off Jena and Kevin and the truck barreling towards them.

Mike glanced down and saw that the green glow was now circling the ice shack! "What is that?" He said out loud. As the cracks in the ice grew bigger the shack began to tip. One edge of the ice the shack was on was now a couple feet higher than the ice of the river. As Jena reached the shack, Mike and Sam reached and pull her over the ice edge. Kevin jumped over and slid into the side of the shack just as the truck slammed sideways into the raised ice! The force of the truck hitting it, sent everyone at the shack tumbling. They got up to watch the cab of the truck sinking into the river!

"Hey! We're floating!" Nicole yelled.

The force of the truck had broken the shack free of the river ice and the shack was moving on its ice island with the current towards Great Falls!

"We're going to go over the falls!" Ashley screamed.

"Calm down," Billy said not really knowing what to do.

"Look!" Mike exclaimed pointing towards the water where the truck had gone down. A large green hump was sticking out of the water!

"What is that?" Sam yelled above the roar of Great Falls, which was getting louder and louder as the shack moved closer and closer to the falls!

No one answered. The others just kept staring at the dam ahead.

Suddenly a giant green head shot out of the water right where they'd been looking! The beast's body rose out of the water and peered down from high above them. Its open mouth full of sharp teeth and a long tongue that darted quickly in and out of an ugly, distorted face with only one eye open! The other eye was shut tight and looked badly bruised.

"It's going to attack!" shouted a voice that seemed to come from the roof of the shack.

Billy and the kids all raced into the shack as the beast lunged at them, its huge head following them into the shack!

"No Little Turtle!" the voice from the roof cried.

The beast shrieked in pain. Billy looked out the window and could see the handle of a small white knife sticking out of the giant eels body. There was the thud of something landing on the ice outside the shack but Billy looked and there was nothing there!

"Quick, Red Feather...use an ice spear!"

"Can't break it, Little Turtle." came back a grunting voice.

The Beast's head was now darting into every corner of the shack. It's long tongue brushed against Kevin's face and then wrapped itself around Nicole, but Billy and Mike held her arms to keep from being dragged out of the shack!

A strong wind suddenly began to whistle through the open boards on the shack walls. Mike looked out the window and saw the hanging fish swaying back and forth. It began thumping against the side of the shack. The flutter of wings soon was heard over the shack followed by a constant chipping sound.

"Good, Yellowbeak! I've got it!" the voice on the roof yelled.

A huge icicle came hurtling down from the roof and ran right through the eel's neck! The beast shrieked in pain and quickly pulled its head out of the shack. Green ooze covered the ice and everything outside as the huge body of the eel deflated like a flat tire and slid into the water! Billy emerged from the shack with the kids but the ooze was so slippery everyone was falling down.

"Look!" screamed Jena, pointing ahead. "We're going to go over the falls!"

"Quick! Everybody back inside the shack!" yelled Billy as the kids and Loni scrambled through the door and Billy shut it behind them.

There was a loud thump and sudden stop as the shack slammed against the dam. Everyone was thrown forward against the door. The shack began to tilt forward but for now it was stopped by the thick piece of ice the shack was floating on and the top of the dam.

"We've got to do something pretty quick!" Billy told them. "The shack can't take this pounding against the dam."

Billy and Mike could look out the window and see that there was about five feet of open water between the ice the shack was floating on and the ice on the river. They could see the Whistlestop through the window. There were several cars including McBean's cruiser and the town truck on shore with a lot of townspeople and Mike and Sam's dog Christy out on the ice.

"I've got an idea," Mike told Billy as he opened the door and began making his way along the shack wall outside by holding onto the pegs Billy used to hang his fish on.

"Hold onto Loni's collar, Kevin." Mike yelled. "I'll be right back." Mike reached down and lifted the heavy shack towrope from its peg and made his way back to the door. Mike tied the end of the rope to Loni's collar as Kevin held the dog.

"Loni doesn't swim very well, Mike." Kevin said.

"It's our only chance, Kevin. Come outside with Loni but hold on to her collar with one hand and one of the wall pegs with the other. I'll be with you."

Mike, Kevin and the dog made their way slowly outside.

"Tell your dad to call Loni, Kevin."

Kevin yelled and Mr. McMahon hollered for Loni to come to him, but the dog just stood at the edge of the ice afraid to jump into the fast moving water. The townspeople were afraid to come closer...afraid that the ice was too thin. Then Christy broke from the crowd and came right to the edge of the river ice, only about five feet from Loni and began barking at her. Loni hesitated then jumped into the water. When she got to the other side, she clawed frantically at the ice trying to pull herself up but the current kept pulling her towards the falls as Christy kept barking!

The shack walls began to creak and distort. Nails popped out and the sidewall boards began falling off the framing and going over the falls! The roof sagged under the weight of the ice and snow and the failing support structure. It looked as though the shack would break up at any moment and they would all go over the dam!

Christy's barking stopped as she bit into Loni's collar, her claws gripping the ice for traction. Both dogs worked to get Loni out of the water. With one final effort Loni was up and the two dogs were racing towards the crowd. Mr. Marsh helped Greeley untie the rope from Loni's collar and tie it to the bumper of the town truck. Greeley signaled Net to pull the truck out onto the ice far enough upriver to take the slack out of the rope and stop the shack from going over the falls. By this time the town fire truck had arrived. Two of the firemen carried a ladder out to the shack using the towrope as a safety line. They placed the ladder over the open water, but by this time the end tied to the shack wall was very weak. Quickly the firemen helped the kids across one by one. Billy was the last and no sooner did he reach safety than the framework of the shack collapsed and went crashing over the falls! The towrope now had only one broken piece of board tied to the end of it. The two dogs had come back onto the ice where the kids were. Both of them began the violent shaking that dogs do when they try to dry themselves.

"Something came off Christy," Ashley said.

"Just a leaf," Kevin answered as he watched it float back into the river.

When Jena was seen running towards her mother and father, and that all the kids were safe, the crowd on the shore began to clap. That is all except for Greeley and Net who called to Billy; "Don't forget your promise!"

"Forget it!" The shack is gone. I don't need you guys anymore!"

Ma Mitchell wagged her finger at Billy, "That's not right! A promise is a promise!"

"I know, Ma, your right. But with my shack gone there goes half of next year's money. And if I show them my best fishing hole I won't be able to make a living!"

"You should have thought about that before you made the promise, Billy."

Billy just grunted something no one understood.

"I'd help fix the tip-ups if you'd let me feed the eagle, Mr. White Fox," Sam offered.

"I don't need a lot of help with the tip-ups, Sam. But maybe there is something else you can help me with. It'll be a while, though. Can't fish again till the ice goes."

"That's okay...just tell me when."

Almost three weeks went by before the ice broke up on the river. Otis Miller was busy building a new bait shack for Billy behind the Whistlestop. Billy came down to the wharf to see how Otis was doing. He passed the kids waiting at the bus stop once again. Mike, Sam, Nicole, Ashley, Kevin and Jena all followed Billy onto the wharf.

"Looks good, Otis. Think you'll have it done in a couple weeks?"

"Yeah, if you can keep those two off my back!" Otis said pointing at Greeley and Net who were fishing off the wharf as usual.

"Don't bother the help, you two!" Billy yelled at them.

"We won't bother Otis if you keep your promise, Billy. The ice is out. When you going to take us to your famous fishin' hole?"

"Soon, Greeley...soon!" Billy said softly.

"When?" Net shot back.

"Couple of days."

"We'll hold you to it, Billy."

"Can we come to?" Kevin asked.

"Okay," Billy answered. "If these two know the whole town will know anyway."

Billy saw Sam playing with Christy in front of his house as he drove by. He stopped the truck and spoke to Sam.

"Sam, I'll let you feed Swift Wing, but first I need you to do a favor for me."

"Sure, Mr. White Fox, what is it?"

Billy sat down and explained what he needed him to do and Sam smiled and nodded his head in agreement.

Two days later Sam woke up early and left the house. Except for a paperboy delivering the morning paper on his bike, Main Street was empty as Sam made his way north. He walked up Main Street to the end and began following the footpath north along the riverbank. Later he came to the place Billy had talked about. The river was wide and there were a lot of big rocks gathered together that jutted out into the river. Sam walked out on the rocks and found the large bucket that Billy said would be there. He sat down between the rocks and waited. It seemed to take a long time, but finally he could see a group of people coming up the path. There was Billy, Greeley, Net, his brother Mike and all his cousins. They were loaded with fishing gear. Sam crouched down between the rocks so no one would see him.

"Where's Sam?" Kevin asked.

"Probably still sleeping," Mike answered. "His door was shut tight when I left."

"This is it!" Billy said. "Better bait your hooks!"

"You sure this is it, Billy? Don't look like anything special to me."

"What did you expect, Greeley? It's just a good fishing hole. Got to let your hook drift in front of those rocks...that's where the big fish are." Billy answered.

One by one the fishing lines were thrown into the water. Mike's was the first to drift in front of the rocks. Shortly, Mike felt a tug on his line and started to reel in. The fish seemed heavy as he drew it closer to shore, but not a lot of fight.

Everyone was excited as Mike held up a large bass.

"That's a keeper!" Net noted.

Now everyone was trying to angle his or her line in front of the big rocks. One by one those who succeeded pulled in a big fish until Net noticed how little fight his fish had. He looked closely at his fish.

"Hey! This fish is almost dead!"

Greeley had baited his hook a second time but his cast fell well short of the rocks. He started to reel in his line to cast again when his pole bent almost in half.

"Got something!" he yelled. But when he lifted it from the water it was only a small branch with one green leaf.

Everyone laughed, but it only made Greeley angry. He took the leaf and threw it in the direction of the kids. It landed on Kevin's tackle box. As soon as Greeley had thrown the leaf, Kevin's pole bent over. His bobber was only a few feet from shore.

"Wow! It's a big one!" Kevin said excitedly. The bass jumped three times before Kevin dared to start reeling again. Mike had to use a net to land it, afraid that the fish was too heavy and might snap the line when lifted out of the water.

Net looked down at the leaf that was still stuck to the side of Kevin's tackle box. "Leafs still green. Wonder why? This time of year they're all dead."

"Some things are preserved for a long time under water. No oxygen to make them age." Greeley said boastfully.

"Your so smart, Greeley. Don't know why you never became president," Billy laughed.

No sooner had Kevin dropped his line in the river, he got another strike! Net had forgotten all about his half dead fish. Everyone began to crowd around Kevin trying to get their line close to his. The wind began to ripple the water. No fishing line was being cast out beyond the rocks that Sam was hiding in. Sam listened to the wind echoing off the rocks all around him. It sounded like two people arguing.

"Looks like a great day for fishing, Red Feather. Too bad we can't show them how."

"You and your magic leaf! If you'd have just accepted the shaman's long path, we'd still be fishing!"

"No Red Feather, we killed the giant eel with a spear of frozen water! We are great warriors!"

"You never give in Little Turtle!"

Sam wondered where the voices were coming from but dared not raise his head to look around and stayed hidden in the rocks until everyone left. He stopped behind the Whistlestop on the way home and had a good laugh with Billy at how they'd fooled Greeley and Net.

Billy paused and began scratching his head; "I never caught fish there as big as what Kevin landed. I know it wasn't from the bucket."

Sam left and walked up Beaver Pond Road and stopped at Kevin and Jena's house. "What did you do with the leaf on your tackle box, Kev?"

"I threw it back in the river. It was all wet. Why? Don't you want to ask me how I caught those big fish?"

"No. I guess not," Sam replied, not wanting to tell about the voices for fear his cousin would think he was crazy.

Sam joined the same excited group at the same spot the next morning. The wind seemed stronger that day and carried the same voices that Sam heard among the rocks.

"Look Little Turtle, the Spirit Of The Wind makes ripples on the water! It is another good day for fishing!"

"There is no leaf. They won't catch any fish here. Why did you say Spirit Of The Wind? Do you now believe in spirits without eyes, Red Feather? Why didn't you say so before? We'd still be fishing!"

"But I still don't believe in that silly magic leaf!"

"But you do Red Feather. It is as Manyfeathers said. If you believe in all the spirits then you will always grow. Your leaf will be forever green."

"You really are a shaman, Little Turtle!"

"Quiet, Red Feather, you're scaring the fish."

Billy smiled as the rest fished quietly, all pretending not to hear the voices for fear their friends would think they were crazy. No one caught any fish that day, not even a nibble. But no one complained, not even Greeley or Net. They watched the wind turn the river into a sea of shimmering silver and whisper through the newly clothed branches of fluttering spring leaves on the birch and maple trees. It was as if the spirits were saying, "The long Moon Of Snow Blinding is over. The green leaf is here again. It always comes back."

Printed in the United States
29743LVS00002B/403-429